NGAIO MARSH

ENTER A MURDERER

HarperCollinsPublishers

HarperCollins *Publishers*
77-85 Fulham Palace Road
Hammersmith, London W6 8JB
www.**fireandwater**.com

This paperback edition published 2001
1

First published in Great Britain by
Geoffrey Bles 1935

Copyright Ngaio Marsh 1935

ISBN 978 0 00 794467 5

Printed in Great Britain by
Clays Ltd, St Ives plc

Enter a Murderer

Dame Ngaio Marsh was born in New Zealand in 1895 and died in February 1982. She wrote over 30 detective novels and many of her stories have theatrical settings, for Ngaio Marsh's real passion was the theatre. She was both actress and producer and almost single-handedly revived the New Zealand public's interest in the theatre. It was for this work that she received what she called her 'damery' in 1966.

CONTENTS

FOREWORD

When I showed this manuscript to my friend, Chief Detective-Inspector Alleyn, of the Criminal Investigation Department, he said:

"It's a perfectly good account of the Unicorn case, but isn't it usual in detective stories to conceal the identity of the criminal?"

I looked at him coldly.

"Hopelessly *vieux jeu*, my dear Alleyn. Nowadays the identity of the criminal is always revealed in the early chapters.

"In that case," he said, "I congratulate you."

I was not altogether delighted.

Chapter 1

PROLOGUE TO A PLAY

On May 25th Arthur Surbonadier, whose real name was Arthur Simes, went to visit his uncle, Jacob Saint, whose real name was Jacob Simes. Jacob was an actor before he went into management and had chosen Saint as his stage name, and stuck to it for the rest of his life. He made bad jokes about it—"I'm no Saint"—and wouldn't allow his nephew to adopt it when he in turn took to the boards. "Only one Saint in the profession," he roared out. "Call yourself what you like, Arthur, but keep off my grass. I'll start you off at the Unicorn and I'll leave you the cash— or most of it. If you're a bad actor you won't get the parts—that's business."

As Arthur Surbonadier ("Surbonadier" had been suggested by Stephanie Vaughan) walked after the footman towards his uncle's library, he remembered his conversation. He was not a bad actor. He was an adequate actor. He was, he told himself, a damn' good actor. He tried to stiffen himself for the encounter. A damn' good actor with personality. He would dominate Jacob Saint. He would, if necessary, use that final weapon—the weapon that Saint knew nothing about. The footman opened the library door.

"Mr Surbonadier, sir."

Arthur Surbonadier walked in.

Jacob Saint was sitting at his ulta-modern desk in his ultra-modern chair. A cubistic lamp lit up the tight rolls of fat at the back of his neck. His grey and white check jacket revealed the muscles of his back. His face was turned away from Surbonadier. Wreaths of cigar smoke rose above his pink head. The room smelt of cigar smoke and the scent he used—it was specially made for him, that scent, and none of his ladies—not even Janet Emerald —had ever been given a flask of it.

9

"Sit down, Arthur," he rumbled. "Have a cigar; I'll talk to you in a moment."

Arthur Surbonadier sat down, refused the cigar, lit a cigarette, and fidgeted. Jacob Saint wrote, grunted, thumped a blotter and swung round in his steel chair.

He was like a cartoon of a theatre magnate. He was as if he played his own character, with his enormous red dewlaps, his coarse voice, his light blue eyes and his thick lips.

"What d'yer want, Arthur?" he said and waited.

"How are you, Uncle Jacob? Rheumatism better?"

"It isn't rheumatism, it's gout, and it's bloody. What d'yer want?"

"It's about the new show at the Unicorn." Surbonadier hesitated, and again Saint waited. "I—I don't know if you've seen the change in the casting."

"I have."

"Oh!"

"Well?"

"Well," said Surbonadier, with a desperate attempt at lightness, "do you approve of it, uncle?"

"I do."

"I don't."

"What the hell does that matter?" asked Jacob Saint. Surbonadier's heavy face whitened. He tried to act the part of himself dominant, himself in control of the stage. Mentally he fingered his weapon.

"Originally," he said, "I was cast for Carruthers. I can play the part and play it well. Now it's been given to Gardener—to Master Felix, whom everybody loves so much."

"Whom Stephanie Vaughan loves so much."

"That doesn't arise," said Surbonadier. His lips trembled. With a kind of miserable exultation he felt his anger welling up.

"Don't be childish, Arthur," rumbled Saint, "and don't come whining to me. Felix Gardener plays Carruthers because he is a better actor than you are. He probably gets Stephanie Vaughan for the same reason. He's got more sex appeal. You're cast for the Beaver. It's a very showy part and they've taken it away from old Barclay Crammer, who would have done it well enough."

"I tell you I'm not satisfied. I want you to make the alteration. I want 'Carruthers'."

"You won't get it. I told you before you'd ever faced the foots that our relationship was not going to be used to jack you up into star parts. I gave you your chance, and you wouldn't have got that if I wasn't your uncle. Now it's up to you." He stared dully at his nephew and then swung his chair towards the desk. "I'm busy," he added. Surbonadier wetted his lips and crossed to him.

"You've bullied me," he said, "all my life. You paid for my education because it suited your vanity to do it, and because you like power."

"Spoken deliberately—comes down-stage slowly! Quite the little actor, aren't you?"

"You've got to get rid of Felix Gardener!"

Jacob Saint for the first time gave his nephew his whole attention. His eyes protruded slightly. He thrust his head forward—it was a trick that was strangely disconcerting and it had served him well when dealing with harder men than Surbonadier.

"Try that line of talk again," he said very quietly, "and you're finished. Now get out."

"Not yet." Surbonadier gripped the top of the desk and cleared his throat. "I know too much about you," he said at last. "More than you realize. I know why you—why you paid Mortlake two thousand." They stared at each other. A dribble of cigar smoke escaped through Saint's half-open lips. When he spoke it was with venomous restraint.

"So we thought we'd try an odd spot of blackmail, did we?" His voice had thickened. "What have you been doing, you——?"

"Did you never miss a letter you had from him last February—when—when I was——"

"When you were my guest. By God, my money's been well spent on you, Arthur!"

"Here's a copy." Surbonadier's shaking hand went to his pocket. He could not take his eyes off Saint. There was something automaton-like about him. Saint glanced at the paper and dropped it.

"If there's any more of this"—his voice rose to a shocking, raucous yell—"I'll have you up for blackmail. I'll ruin you. You'll never get another shop in London. You hear that?"

"I'll do it." Surbonadier backed away, actually as though he feared he would be attacked. "I'll do it." His hand was on the door. Jacob Saint stood up. He was six feet tall and enormous. He should have dominated the room— he was much the better animal of the two. Yet Surbonadier, unhealthy, too soft, and shaking visibly, had about him an air of sneaking mastery.

"I'm off," he said.

"No," said Saint. "No. Sit down again. I'll talk."

Surbonadier went back to his chair.

On the night of June 7th, after the first performance of *The Rat and the Beaver*, Felix Gardener gave a party in his flat in Sloane Street. He had invited all the other members of the cast, even old Susan Max, who got buccaneerish over the champagne, and talked about the parts she had played with Julius Knight in Australia. Janet Emerald, the "heavy" of the play, listened to her with an air of gloomy profundity. Stephanie Vaughan was very much the leading lady, very tranquil, very gracious, carelessly kind to everyone and obviously pliant to Felix Gardener himself. Nigel Bathgate, the only journalist at the party and an old Cambridge friend of Felix, wondered if he and Miss Vaughan were about to announce their engagement. Surely their mutual attentiveness meant something more than mere theatrical effusion. Arthur Surbonadier was there, rather too friendly with everybody, thought Nigel, who disliked him; and J. Barclay Crammer, who disliked him even more, glared at Surbonadier across the table. Dulcie Deamer, the *jeune fille* of the play, was also the *jeune fille* of the party. And Howard Melville ran her a good second in registering youthful charm, youthful bashfulness and something else that was genuinely youthful and rather pleasing. Jacob Saint was there, loudly jovial and jovially loud. "My company, my actors, my show," he seemed to shout continually, and indeed did. To the playwright, who was present and submissive, Saint actually referred as "my author." The playwright remained submissive. Even George Simpson, the stage manager, was present, and it was he who began the conversation that Nigel was to recall a few weeks later, and relate to his friend, Detective-Inspector Alleyn.

"That business with the gun went off all right, Felix," Simpson said, "though I must say I was nervous about it. I hate a fake."

"Was it all right from the front?" asked Surbonadier, turning to Nigel Bathgate.

"What do you mean? asked Nigel. "What business with the gun?"

"My God, he doesn't even remember it!" sighed Felix Gardener. "In the third act, my dear chap, I shoot the Beaver—Arthur—Mr. Surbonadier at close range and he falls down dead."

"Of course I remember that," said Nigel, rather nettled. "It was perfectly all right. Most convincing. The gun went off."

"The gun went off!" screamed Miss Dulcie Deamer hilariously. "Did you hear him, Felix?"

"The gun didn't go off," said the stage manager. "That's just the point. I fire another off in the prompt corner and Felix jerks his hand. You see, he shoots the Beaver at close range—actually presses the barrel of the revolver into his waistcoat, so we can't use a blank—it would scorch his clothes. The cartridges that the Beaver loads his gun with are all duds—empty shells."

"I'm damned glad you don't," said Arthur Surbonadier. "I loathe guns and I sweat blood in that scene. The price one pays," he added heavily, "for being an actor." He glanced at his uncle, Jacob Saint.

"Oh, for Heaven's sake!" muttered J. Barclay Crammer in a bitterly scornful aside to Gardener.

"It's your own gun, isn't it, Felix? he said aloud.

"Yes," said Felix Gardener. "It was my brother's—went all through Flanders with him." His voice deepened.

"I'm not leaving it in the theatre. Too precious. Here it is." A little silence fell upon the company as he produced a service revolver and laid it on the table.

"It makes the play seem rather paltry," said the author of the play.

They spoke no more of the gun.

On the morning of June 14th, when *The Rat and the Beaver* had run a week to full houses, Felix Gardener sent Nigel Bathgate two complimentary tickets for the stalls. Angela North, who does not come into this story, was away from London, so Nigel rang up Scotland Yard and asked for his friend, Chief Detective-Inspector Alleyn.

"Are you doing anything to-night?" he said.

"What do you want me to do?" said the voice in the receiver.

"How cautious you are!" said Nigel. "I've got a couple of seats for the show at the Unicorn. Felix Gardener gave them to me."

"You do know a lot of exciting people!" remarked the inspector. "I'll come with pleasure. Dine with me first, won't you?"

"You dine with me. It's my party."

"Really? This promises well."

"That's splendid!" said Nigel. "I'll pick you up at a quarter to seven."

"Right you are. I'm due for a night off," said the voice. "Thank you, Bathgate. Good-bye."

"Hope you enjoy it," said Nigel, but the receiver had gone dead.

At cocktail-time on that same day, June 14th, Arthur Surbonadier called on Miss Stephanie Vaughan at her flat in Shepherd's Market and asked her to marry him. It was not the first time he had done so. Miss Vaughan felt herself called upon to use all her professional and personal *savoir-faire*. The scene needed some handling and she gave it her full attention.

"Darling," she said, taking her time over lighting a cigarette and quite unconsciously adopting the best of her

14

six by-the-mantelpiece poses. "Darling, I'm so terribly, terribly upset by all this. I feel I'm to blame. I *am* to blame."

Surbonadier was silent. Miss Vaughan changed her pose. He knew quite well, through long experience, what her next pose would be, and equally well that it would charm him as though he were watching her for the first time. Her voice would drop. She would purr. She did purr.

"Arthur darling, I'm all nervy. This piece has exhausted my vitality. I don't know where I am. You must be patient with me. I feel I'm incapable of loving anybody." She let her arms fall limply to her sides and then laid one hand delicately on her *décolletage* for him to look at. "Quite incapable," she added on a drifting sigh.

"Even of loving Felix Gardener?" said Surbonadier.

"Ah—Felix!" Miss Vaughan gave her famous three-cornered smile, lifted her shoulders a little, looked meditative and resigned. She managed to convey a world of something or another, quite beyond her control.

"It comes to this," said Surbonadier. "Has Gardener" —he paused and looked away from her—"has Gardener cut me out?"

"My sweet, *what* an Edwardianism. Felix talks one of my languages. You talk another."

"I wish to God," said Surbonadier, "that you would confine yourself to plain English. I can talk that as well as he. I love you. I want you. Does that come into any of your languages?"

Miss Vaughan sank into a chair and clasped her hands.

"Arthur," she said, "I must have my freedom. I can't be closed in emotionally. Felix *gives* me something."

"The hell he does," said Surbonadier. He too sat down, and such was the habit of the stage, he sat down rather stagily. His hands shook with genuine emotion, though, and Stephanie Vaughan eyed him and knew it.

"Arthur," she said, "you must forgive me, darling. I'm very attached to you and I hate hurting you, but—if you can—leave off wanting me. Don't ask me to marry you— I might say 'Yes' and make you even more unhappy than you are now."

15

Even while she spoke she knew she had made a false step. He had moved quickly to her side and taken her in his arms.

"I'd risk the unhappiness," he muttered. "I want you so much." He pressed his face into her neck. She shivered a little. Unseen by him her face expressed a kind of exultant disgust. Her hands were on his hair. Suddenly she thrust him away.

"No, no, no," she said. "Don't! Leave me alone. Can't you see I'm sick of it all? Leave me alone."

In all the "bad men" parts he had played Surbonadier had never looked quite so evil as he did at that moment.

"I'm damned if I'll leave you alone," he said. "I'm not going to be kicked out. I don't care if you hate me. I want you, and by God I'll have you."

He took her by the wrists. She did not attempt to resist him. They stared, full of antagonism, into each other's faces.

Distantly an electric bell sounded and at once her moment of surrender, if it had been a moment of surrender, was past.

"That's the front door," she said. "Let me go, Arthur." She had to struggle before she could break away from him, and he was still beside her, in a state of rather blatant agitation, when Felix Gardener walked into the room.

Chapter II

"OVERTURE AND BEGINNERS, PLEASE"

The stage door-keeper of the Unicorn glanced up at the grimy face of the clock—7.10. All the artists were snug in their dressing-rooms now. All, that was, except old Susan Max, who played an insignificant part in the last act and was given a bit of licence by the stage manager. Susan came in about eight.

Footsteps sounded in the alley outside. Old Blair uttered

a kind of groaning sigh peculiar to himself, got creakily off his stool, and peered out into the warmish air. In a moment two men in evening dress stepped into the pool of uncertain light cast by the stage door lamp. Blair moved into the doorway and looked at them in silence.

"Good evening," said the shorter of the two men.

"Evening, sir," said Blair, and waited.

"Can we see Mr. Gardener, do you think? He's expecting us. Mr. Bathgate." He opened a cigarette-case and produced a card. Old Blair took it and shifted his gaze to the taller of the two visitors. "Mr. Alleyn is with me," said Nigel Bathgate.

"Will you wait a moment, please?" said Blair, and holding the card in the palm of his hand as if he were rather ashamed of it, he walked off down the passage.

"That old gentleman had a good look at you," said Nigel Bathgate. He offered his cigarette-case.

"Perhaps he knew me," said Chief Detective-Inspector Alleyn. "I'm famous as anything, you know."

"Are you, now? Too famous, perhaps, to be amused at this sort of thing?" Nigel waved his cigarette in the direction of the passage.

"Not a bit. I'm as simple as I am clever—a lovable trait in my character. An actor in his dressing-room will thrill me to mincemeat. I shall sit and goggle at him, I promise you."

"Felix is more likely to goggle at you. When he gave me a couple of stalls for to-night I told him Angela couldn't come and—I mean," said Nigel hurriedly, "I said I'd ask you, and he was quite startled by the importance of me."

"So he ought to be—all took aback. When your best girl's away ask a policeman. Sensible man, Felix Gardener, as well as a damn' good actor. And I do love a crook play, I do."

"Oh," said Nigel, "I never thought of that. Rather a busman's holiday for you, I'm afraid."

"Not it. Is it the sort where you have to guess the murderer?"

"It is. And you'll look a bit silly if you can't, won't you, inspector?"

"Shut up. I shall bribe this old gentleman to tell me. Here he comes." Old Blair appeared at the end of the passage.

"Will you come this way, please?" he said, without returning to the door.

Nigel and Alleyn stepped inside the stage door of the Unicorn, and at that precise moment Chief Detective-Inspector Alleyn, all unknowingly, walked into one of the toughest jobs of his career.

They at once sensed the indescribable flavour of the working half of a theatre when the nightly show is coming on. The stage door opens into a little realm, strange or familiar, but always apart and shut in. The passage led directly on to the stage, which was dimly lit and smelt of dead scene paint, of fresh grease paint, of glue-size, and of dusty darkness, time out of mind the incense of the playhouse. A pack of scene flats leaned against the wall and a fireman leaned against the outer flat, which was painted to represent a section of a bookcase. A man in shirt sleeves and rubber-soled shoes ran distractedly round the back of the set. A boy carrying a bouquet of sweet peas disappeared into a brightly-lit entry on the right. The flats of the "set" vanished up into an opalescent haze. Beyond them, lit by shaded lamps, the furniture of a library mutely faced the reverse side of the curtain. From behind the curtain came the disturbing and profoundly exciting murmur of the audience, and the immemorial squall of tuning fiddle-strings. Though the prompt entrance another man in shirt sleeves stared into the flies.

" What are you doing with those bloody blues?" he inquired. His voice was deadened by carpets and furniture. Someone far above answered. A switch clicked and the set was suddenly illuminated. A pair of feet appeared above Nigel's face; he looked up and saw dimly the electricians' platform, on which one man stood with his hand on the switch-board and another sat dangling his legs. Blair led them into the bright entry, which turned out to be another passage. Along this passage on the left were the dressing-room doors, the first marked with a tarnished star. From behind all the doors came the sound of muffled voices—cosy, busy, at home. It was very warm. A man with a worried expression hurried round an elbow in the passage. As he passed he looked at them inquisitively.

"That's George Simpson, the stage manager," whispered Nigel importantly. Old Blair knocked on the second door.

There was a pause and then a pleasant baritone voice called:

"Hullo, who is it?"

Blair opened the door two inches and said: "Your visitors, Mr. Gardener."

"What? Oh, yes. Half a second," called the voice. And then to someone inside: "I quite agree with you, old boy, but what can you do? No, don't go." A chair scraped and in a moment the door was opened. "Come in, come in," said Felix Gardener.

They crossed the threshold and Inspector Alleyn found himself, for the first time in his life, in an actor's dressing-room and shaking hands with the actor.

Felix Gardener was not a preposterously good-looking man; not, that is to say, so handsome that the male section of his audience longed at times to give him a kick in the pants. He had, however, the elusive quality of distinction. His straw-coloured hair was thick and lay sleekly on his neatly shaped head. His eyes, scarcely the width of an eye apart, were surprisingly blue, his nose straight and narrow; his mouth, generously large and curiously folded in at the corners, was a joy to newspaper cartoonists. His jaw-line was sharply marked, giving emphasis to a face otherwise rather fine-drawn. He was tall, carried himself beautifully, but not too much like a showman, and he had a really delightful speaking voice, light but resonant. He was said by women to have "It"; by men to be a very decent fellow; and by critics to be an actor of outstanding ability.

"I'm so glad you've come round," he said to Alleyn. "Do sit down. Oh—may I introduce Mr. Barclay Crammer? Mr. Alleyn. Bathgate you've met."

J. Barclay Crammer was a character actor. He was

just sufficiently well known for people to say "Who *is* that man?" when he walked on to the stage, and not quite distinctive enough for them to bother to look him up in the programme. He was dark, full-faced, and a good character actor. He looked bad-tempered, thought Nigel, who had met him once before at Gardener's first-night supper-party.

"Can you all find somewhere to sit?" asked Gardener. He seated himself in front of his dressing-table. Alleyn and Nigel found a couple of arm-chairs.

The room was a blaze of lights and extremely warm. a gas jet protected by an open cage bubbled above the dressing-table, on which stood a mirror and all the paraphernalia of make-up. The room smelt of grease paint. Near the mirror lay a revolver and a pipe. A full-length glass hung on the right-hand wall by a wash-basin. On the left-hand wall a looped-up sheet half covered a collection of suits. Through the wall came the sound of women's voices in the star room.

"So glad you've both come, Nigel," said Gardener. "I never see you nowadays. You journalists are devilish hard to get hold of."

"Not more elusive than you actors," rejoined Nigel, "and not half as slippery as the police. I may tell you it's rather a feather in my cap producing Alleyn to-night."

"I know," agreed Gardener, turning to his mirror and dabbing his face with brown powder. "It makes me quite nervous. Do you realise, J.B., that Mr Alleyn is a kingpin in the C.I.D.?"

"Really?" intoned Mr. Barclay Crammer deeply. He hesitated a moment and then added with rather ponderous gaiety: "Makes me even more nervous as I'm one of the villains of the piece. A very, very minor villain," he added with unmistakable bitterness.

"Now, don't tell me you're the murderer," said Alleyn. "It would ruin my evening."

"Nothing so important," said Barclay Crammer. "A little 'cameo part,' the management tells me. And that's throwing roses at it."

He uttered a short, scornful noise which Nigel recognised as part of his stock-in-trade.

A voice outside in the passage called:

"Half-hour, please. Half-hour, please."

"I must be off," said Mr. Crammer, sighing heavily. "I'm not made up yet and I begin this revolting piece. Pah!" He rose majestically and made a not unimpressive exit.

"Poor old J.B.'s very disgruntled," said Gardener in an undertone. "He was to play the Beaver and then it was given to Arthur Surbonadier. Great heart-burning, I assure you." He smiled charmingly. "It's a rum life, Nigel," he said.

"You mean they are rum people?" said Nigel.

"Yes—partly. Like children and terribly, terribly like actors. They run too true to type."

"You were not so critical in our Trinity days."

"Don't remind me of my callow youth."

"Youth!" said Alleyn. "You children amuse me. Twenty years ago next month I came down from Oxford. Ah me! Fie fie! Out upon it!"

"All the same," persisted Nigel, "you can't persuade me, Felix, that you are out of conceit with your job."

"That's another matter," said Felix Gardener.

There was a light tap on the door, which opened far enough to disclose a rather fat face, topped by a check cap and garnished with a red spotted handkerchief. It was accompanied by an unmistakable gust of alcohol, only partially disguised by violet cachous.

"Hullo—hullo, Arthur, come in," said Gardener pleasantly, but without any great enthusiasm.

"So sorry," said the face unctuously. "Thought you were alone, old man. Wouldn't intrude for the world."

"Rot!" said Gardener. "Do come in and shut the door. There's a hellish draught in this room."

"No, no, it's not important. Just that little matter of—— I'll see you later." The face withdrew and the door was shut, very gently.

"That's Arthur Surbonadier," Gardener explained to

Alleyn. "He's pinched J.B.'s part and thinks I've pinched his. Result, J.B. hates him and he hates me. That's what I mean about actors."

"Oh!" said Nigel, with youthful profundity, "Jealousy."

"And whom do you hate?" asked Alleyn lightly.

"I?" Gardener said. "I'm at the top of this particular tree and can afford to be generous. I dare say I'll get like it sooner or later."

"Do you think Surbonadier a good actor?" asked Nigel. Gardener lifted one shoulder.

"He's Jacob Saint's nephew."

"I see. Or do I?"

"Jacob Saint owns six theatres, of which this is one. He gives good parts to Surbonadier. He never engages poor artists. Therefore Surbonadier must be a good actor. I refuse to be more catty than that. Do you know this play?" he said, turning to Alleyn.

"No," said the inspector. "Not a word of it. I have been trying to discover from your make-up whether you are a hero, a racketeer, one of us police, or all three. The pipe on your dressing-table suggests a hero, the revolver a racketeer, and the excellent taste of the coat you are about to put on, a member of my own profession. I deduce, my dear Bathgate, that Mr. Gardener is a hero disguised as a gun-man, and a member of the C.I.D."

"There!" said Nigel triumphantly. He turned proudly to Gardener. For once Alleyn was behaving nicely as a detective.

"Marvellous!" said Gardener.

"You don't mean to tell me I'm right?" said Alleyn.

"Not far out. But I use the revolver as a policeman, the pipe as a gun-man, and don't wear that suit in this piece at all."

"Which only goes to show," said Alleyn, grinning, "that intuition is as good as induction any day." They lit cigarettes and Nigel and Gardener began a long reminiscent yarn about their Cambridge days.

The door opened again and a little dried-up man in an alpaca jacket came in.

"Ready, Mr. Gardener?" he asked, scarcely glancing at the others.

Gardener took off his wrap, and the dresser got a coat from under the sheet and helped him into it. "You need a touch more powder, sir, if I may say so," he remarked. "It's a warm night."

"That gun business all right?" asked Gardener, turning back to the mirror.

"Props says so. Let me give you a brush, if you please, Mr. Gardener."

"Oh, get along with you, Nannie," rejoined Gardener. He submitted good-humouredly to the clothes brush.

"Handkerchief," murmured the dresser, flicking one into the jacket. "Pouch in side pocket. Pipe. Are you right, sir?"

"Right as rain—run along."

"Thank you, sir. Shall I take the weapon to Mr. Surbonadier, sir?"

"Yes. Go along to Mr. Surbonadier's room. My compliments, and will he join these gentlemen as my guests for supper?" He took up the revolver.

"Certainly, sir," said the dresser, and went out.

"Bit of a character, that," said Gardener. "You will sup with me, won't you? I've asked Surbonadier because he dislikes me. It will add piquancy to the dressed crab."

"Quarter hour, please. Quarter hour, please," said the voice outside.

"We'd better go round to the front," said Nigel.

"Plenty of time. I want you to meet Stephanie Vaughan, Alleyn. She's madly keen on criminology and would never forgive me if I hid you." (Alleyn looked politely resigned.) "Stephanie!" Gardener shouted loudly. A muffled voice from beyond the wall sang:

"Hullo—oh?"

"Can I bring visitors in to see you?"

"Of *course*, dar-ling," trilled the voice, histrionically cordial.

"Marvellous woman!" said Gardener. "Let's go."

Behind the tarnished star they found Miss Stephanie Vaughan in a rather bigger room, with thicker carpets, larger chairs, a mass of flowers and an aproned dresser. She received them with much gaiety gave them cigarettes and dealt out her charm lavishly, with perhaps an extra libation for Gardener and a hint, thought Nigel of something more subtly challenging in her manner towards Inspector Alleyn. Even with blue grease on her eyelids and scarlet grease on her nostrils, she was a very lovely woman, with beautifully groomed hair, enormous eyes, and a heart-shaped face. Her three-cornered smile was famous. She began to talk shop—Alleyn's shop—to the inspector, and asked him if he had read H. B. Irving's book on famous criminals. He said he had, and thought it jolly good. She asked him if he had read other books on criminals and psychology; if he had read Freud, if he had read Ernest Jones. Mr. Alleyn said he thought them all jolly good. Nigel felt nervous.

" I've saturated myself in the literature of crime," said Miss Vaughan. " I've tried to understand, deep down, the psychology of the criminal. I'm greedy for more. Tell me of more books to read, Mr. Alleyn."

" Have you read Edgar Wallace?" asked Alleyn. " He's jolly good."

There was a nasty silence, and then Miss Vaughan decided to let loose her lovely laugh. It rang out—a glorious, bubbling cascade of joyousness. Gardener and Nigel joined in, the latter unconvincingly. Gardener flung his head back and shouted. He put his hand lightly on Stephanie Vaughan's shoulder.

Then quite suddenly they were aware that the door had been flung open and that Arthur Surbonadier was standing in the room. With one hand he held on to the door—with the other he fumbled at the spotted neckerchief below his scrubby beard. His mouth was half open and he seemed to be short of breath. At last he spoke.

" Quite a jolly little party," he said. His voice was thick and they saw how his lips trembled. They stopped short in their laughter, Gardener still with his hand on that lovely shoulder, Stephanie Vaughan open-mouthed and frozen into immobility—rather as though they were posing for a theatrical photograph. There was a quite appalling little silence.

"Charming picture," said Surbonadier. "All loving and bright. Mayn't I know the joke?"

"The joke," said Alleyn quickly, "was a bad one—of mine."

"The cream of the jest," said Surbonadier, "is on me. Stephanie will explain it to you. You're the detective, aren't you?"

Gardener and Nigel both started talking. Nigel heard himself introduce Alleyn. Gardener was saying something about his supper-party. Alleyn had got to his feet and was offering Miss Vaughan a cigarette. She took it without moving her gaze off Surbonadier, and Alleyn lit it for her.

"I'm sure we ought to go round to the front," he said. "Don't let's miss the first scene, Nigel—I can't bear to be late."

He took Nigel by the arm, said something courteous to Miss Vaughan, shook Gardener's hand, and propelled Nigel towards the door.

"Don't let me drive you away," said Surbonadier, without moving from the doorway. "I've come to see the fun. Came to see Gardener really, and found him—having his fun."

"Arthur!" Stephanie Vaughan spoke for the first time.

"Well," said Surbonadier loudly, "I've made up m' mind to stop the fun—see? No reason why you shouldn't hear"—he turned slightly towards Nigel. "You're a journalist. Literary man. Here's a surprise—Gardener's a literary man, too."

"Arthur, you're tight," said Gardener. He moved towards Surbonadier, who took a step towards him. Alleyn seized his chance and shoved Nigel through the door.

"Good-bye for the moment," he called. "See you after the show"—and in a second or two they were back on the stage staring at one another.

"That was pretty beastly," said Nigel.

"Yes," said Alleyn. "Come on."

"The brute's drunk," said Nigel.

"Yes," said Alleyn. "This way."

They crossed the stage and made for the exit door, standing aside to let an elderly woman come in; they heard old Blair say: "'Evening, Miss Max." As they went out a voice in the passage behind them called:

"Overture and beginners, please. Overture and beginners, please."

Chapter III

DEATH OF THE BEAVER

"It's amazing to me," said Nigel, in the second interval, "how that fellow Surbonadier can play a part in the state he's in. You'd never guess he was tight now, would you?"

"I *think* I would have known," said Alleyn. "From where we are you can see his eyes—they don't quite focus."

"I call it a damn' good performance," said Nigel.

"Yes," murmured Alleyn. "Yes. You've seen the piece before, haven't you?"

"Reviewed it," said Nigel, rather grandly.

"Has Surbonadier's reading of the part altered at all?" Nigel turned and stared at his friend. "Well," he said slowly, "now I come to think of it I believe it has. It's —it's sort of more intense. I mean in that last scene with Felix, when they were alone on the stage. What is it he says to Felix? Something about getting him?"

"'I'll get you, Carruthers,'" quoted Alleyn, with an uncannily just rendering of Surbonadier's thick voice. "'I'll get you, and just when you least expect it!'"

"Good Lord, Alleyn, what a memory you've got!" said Nigel, very startled.

"I've never before seen anything on the stage that impressed me so deeply."

"All carried away like," jibed Nigel, but Alleyn refused to laugh.

"It was uncanny," he said. "The atmosphere of the dressing-room intensified on the stage. Intensified and bigger than life, like emotion in a nightmare. And then he said: 'You think I'm bluffing, playing a part, don't you?' And 'Carruthers'—Gardener, you know—said: 'I think you're bluffing, Beaver—yes. But if you're not—look out!'"

"You're a damn' good mimic, inspector."

"Clap-trap stuff it is really," said Alleyn uneasily.

"What's the matter with you?"

"I don't know. Got the ooble-boobles. Let's have a drink."

They went to the bar. The inspector was very silent and read his programme. Nigel looked at his curiously. He felt apologetic about the horribly uncomfortable scene in the dressing-room and wondered very much what was brewing between Gardener, Surbonadier and Miss Vaughan.

"I suppose old Felix has cut that bounder out?" he ventured.

"Yes," said Alleyn. "Oh, yes—that, of course." The warning bell set up its intolerable racket. "Come on," said Alleyn. "Don't let's miss any of it." He fidgeted while Nigel finished his drink, and led the way back to their stalls.

"The supper-party won't be much fun, I'm afraid," said Nigel.

"Oh—the supper-party. Perhaps it'll be off."

"Perhaps. What'll we do if it's on? Apologise and get out?"

"Wait and see."

"Helpful suggestion!"

"I don't think the supper-party will happen."

"Here she goes," remarked Nigel, as the lights slowly died away, leaving the auditorium in thick-populated darkness.

At the bottom of the blackness in front of them a line of light appeared. It widened, and in a silence so complete that the sound of the pulleys could be heard, the curtain rose on the last act of *The Rat and the Beaver*.

It opened with a scene between the Beaver (Surbonadier), his cast-off mistress (Janet Emerald), and her mother (Susan Max). They were all involved in the opium trade. One of their number had been murdered. They had suspected him of being a stool-pigeon in the employ of Carruthers, *alias* the Rat (Felix Gardener). Miss Emerald threatened, Miss Max snivelled, Surbonadier snarled. He took a revolver from his pocket and loaded it while they watched him significantly.

" *What are you going to do?*" whispered Janet Emerald " *Pay a little visit to Mister Carruthers.*"

The stage was blacked out for a quick change.

Carruthers (Felix Gardener) was discovered in his library among the leather chairs that Nigel and Alleyn had seen from the wings. It was still uncertain, to all but the wariest playgoer, whether he was the infamous Rat, organiser of illicit drug traffic, agent of the Nazis, enemy of the people, or the heroic servant of the British Secret Service. He sat at his desk and rapped out a letter on the typewriter, the keyboard of which was not visible.

" He pounds away at the letter Q," whispered Nigel full of inside knowledge.

To Gardener came Jennifer (Stephanie Vaughan) passionately in love with him, believing him false, fascinated in spite of her nobler self, by the famous Felix charm. Miss Vaughan did this sort of thing remarkably well, the audience was enchanted, especially as at any moment the bookcase might slide back revealing the Butler (J. Barclay Crammer), whom they knew to be a gun-man of gun-men. It was, as Nigel had remarked in reviewing the play, a generous helping out of the old stock-pot, but Felix Gardener and Stephanie Vaughan played it with subtlety and restraint. The lines were sophisticated if the matter was melodramatic, and " it went." Even when the sliding bookcase slid and the gun-man did seize Miss Vaughan by her lovely elbows and pinion her, he did it, as it were, on the turn of an epigram, since as well as being a butler and a gun-man he was also an Etonian.

Miss Vaughan was borne off registering a multitude of conflicting emotions and Felix Gardener remained wrapped in the closest inscrutability. He took out his pipe, filled and lit it, gave a little audible sigh and sank into one of the leather chairs. " Isn't he marvellous!" breathed a woman's voice from behind Nigel. Nigel smiled a superior but tolerant smile and glanced at Alleyn. The inspector's dark eyes were fixed on the stage.

" Positively," thought Nigel, more tolerant than ever, " positively old Alleyn's all het up." Then he saw Alleyn's eyebrow perk up and his lips tighten and he himself turned to the stage and experienced an emotional shock.

Surbonadier, in his character of the Beaver, was standing in the upstage entrance facing the audience. With one hand he held on to the door and with the other he fumbled with his spotted neckerchief below his scrubby beard. His mouth was half open and he seemed to be short of breath.

At last he spoke. So complete was the duplication of the scene in the dressing-room that Nigel expected to hear him repeat : " Quite a jolly little party," and got another shock when he said very softly :

" *So the Rat's in his hole at last!*"

" *Beaver:*" whispered Felix Gardener. It was a line that most actors would have played for a laugh. Few actors could have played it otherwise, but Felix Gardener did. He made it sound horrible.

The Beaver came downstage. His right hand now held a revolver. " *You're not a killer, Rat,*" he said. " *I am. Put 'em up.*"

Gardener's hands went slowly above his head. Surbonadier patted him all over, still covering him with the gun. Then he backed away. He began to arraign Gardener. The intensity of his fury, repressed and controlled apparently by the most stringent effort, touched the audience like venom. The emotional contact between the players and the house was tightened to an almost unendurable tension. Nigel felt profoundly uncomfortable. It seemed to him that this was no fustian scene between the Rat and the Beaver, but a development of the antagonism of two men, indecently played out in public. " Carruthers, the Rat" was his friend Felix Gardener, and the "Beaver" was Arthur Surbonadier, who hated him. The whole business was beastly and he would have liked to look away from it but for the life of him he couldn't do so.

"*Round every corner, Rat, you've waited for me,*" Surbonadier was saying. now. "*Every job I've done this last year you've bitched for me, Rat—Rat. You've mucked round my girl.*" His voice rose hysterically. "*I've had enough. I'm through—I've come to finish it and, by God I've come to finish you:*"

"*Not this evening, Beaver. It's a lovely little plan and I hate to spoil your party, but you see we're not alone.*"

"*What are you saying?*"

"*We're not alone.*" Gardener spoke with the exasperating facetiousness of the popular hero. "*There's a good angel watching over you, Beaver. You're covered, my Beaver.*"

"*Do I look easy?*"

"*You look lovely, my Beaver, but if you don't believe me take a step to your right and glance in the mirror behind me, and I think you'll see the image of the angel that's watching you.*"

Surbonadier moved upstage. His right hand still held the revolver levelled at Gardener, but for a second he shifted his gaze to the mirror above Gardener's head. Then slowly he turned and stared at the upstage entrance. A moment, and Stephanie Vaughan stood in the doorway She too held a revolver, pointed at Surbonadier.

"*Jenny!*" whispered Surbonadier. He dropped his hand and the barrel of the gun shone blue. It hung limply from his fingers and as though in a dream he let Gardener take it from him.

"*Thank you, Jennifer,*" said Gardener. Miss Vaughan, with a little laugh, lowered her gun.

"*You don't have any luck, do you, Beaver?*" she said.

Surbonadier uttered a curious little whinnying sound, turned, and clawed at Gardener's neck, forcing up his chin. Gardener's hand jerked up. The report of the revolver, anticipated by every nerve in the audience, was deafeningly loud. Surbonadier crumpled up and, turning a face that was blank of every expression but that of profound astonishment, fell in a heap at Gardener's feet. So far the acting honours in the scene had been even, but now Felix Gardener surpassed anything that had gone before. His face reflected, horribly, the surprise on Surbonadier's. He stood looking foolishly at the gun in his hand and then let it fall to the floor. He turned, bewildered, and peering at the audience as though asking a question. He looked at the stage exits as if he meditated an escape. Then he gazed at Stephanie Vaughan, who, in her turn, was looking with horror from him to what he had done. When at last he spoke—and his lips moved once or twice before any words were heard—it was with the voice of an automaton. Miss Vaughan replied like an echo. They spoke as though they were talking machines. Gardener kept his gaze fixed on the revolver. Once he made as if he would pick it up, but drew his hand back as though it were untouchable.

"God, that man can act!" said a voice behind Nigel. He woke up to feel Alleyn's hand on his knee.

"Is this the end?" the inspector whispered.

"Yes," said Nigel. "The curtain comes down in a moment."

"Then let's get out."

"What!"

"Let's get out," repeated Alleyn; and then, with a change of voice: "Are you looking for me?"

Their seats were on the aisle. Glancing up, Nigel saw that an usher was bending over his friend.

"Are you Inspector Alleyn, sir?"

"Yes. You want me. I'll come. Get up, Bathgate."

Completely at a loss, Nigel rose and followed Alleyn and the usher up the aisle, into the foyer, and out by a sort of office to the stage door alley. No one spoke until then, when the usher said:

"It's terrible, sir—it's terrible."

"Quite," said Alleyn coldly. "I know."

"Did you guess, sir? Have they all guessed?"

"I don't think so. Is someone going to ask for a doctor? Not that there's any hurry for that."

31

" My Gawd, sir, is he dead?"

" Of course he's dead."

As they approached the stage door old Blair came running out, wringing his hands.

Alleyn walked past him, followed by Nigel. A man in a dinner jacket, his face very white, came down the passage.

" Inspector Alleyn?" he said.

" Here," said Alleyn. " Is the curtain down?"

" I don't think so. Shall I go out in front and ask for a doctor? We didn't realise. I didn't stop the show. Nobody realised—they don't know in front—I don't think they know in front. He said we ought to send for you," the man gabbled on madly. They reached the wings just as the curtain came down; Stephanie Vaughan and Gardener were still on the stage. The applause from the auditorium broke like a storm of hail. Simpson, the stage manager, darted out of the prompt corner. As soon as the fringe of the curtain touched the stage Miss Vaughan screamed and hurled her arms round Gardener's neck. Simpson held back the curtain, looking with horror at Surbonadier, who lay close to his feet. The man in evening dress, who was the business manager, stepped through. The orchestra blared out the first note of the National Anthem, but the man must have held up his hand or spoken to them, because the noise of the one note petered out foolishly. On the stage they heard the business manager speaking to the audience.

" If there is a doctor in front, will he kindly come round to the stage door? Thank you."

The orchestra again struck up the National Anthem. Behind the curtain Alleyn spoke to Simpson.

" Go to the street door and stop anyone from leaving. No one is to go out. You understand? Bathgate, find a telephone and get the Yard. Tell them from me what has happened and ask them to send the usual people. Say I'll want constables." He turned to the business manager, who had come through the curtain. " Show Mr. Bathgate the way to the nearest telephone and then come back here." He knelt down by Surbonadier.

The business manager glanced at Nigel.

" Where's a telephone?" asked Nigel.

" Yes, of course," said the business manager. " I'll show you."

They went together through a door in the proscenium that led to the auditorium, almost colliding with a tall man in a tail coat.

" I'm the doctor," he said. " What's it all about?"

" On the stage," said Nigel, " if you'll go through." The doctor glanced at him and went on to the stage.

In the auditorium the last stragglers were still finding their way out. Some women with their heads together stood with bundles of dust sheets in their arms.

" Get on with your work," said the business manager savagely. " My name's Stavely, Mr.—Mr.——"

" Bathgate," said Nigel.

" Yes, of course. This is a terrible business, Mr Bathgate."

" No one," thought Nigel, " seems to be able to say anything but this."

They crossed the foyer into an office. People were still standing about the entrance and a woman said:

" You're not very clever about taxis, are you, darling?"

Nigel, at the telephone, remembered the Yard number. A man's voice answered him very quickly.

" I'm speaking for Chief Detective-Inspector Alleyn," said Nigel. " There's been an accident at the Unicorn a—a fatal accident. He wants you to send the usual people and constables at once."

" Very good," said the voice. " Did you say fatal accident?"

" Yes," said Nigel, " I think so, and I think——" He stopped, gulped, and then his voice seemed to add of its own accord: " I think it looks like murder."

Chapter IV

ALLEYN TAKES OVER

When Nigel got back to the stage he was surprised to
find little alteration in the scene he had left. He did not
realise how short a time he had been away. The doctor
had finished his examination of Surbonadier's body and
stood looking down at him.

Miss Vaughan was still on the stage. She was sobbing
in the arms of old Susan Max. Felix Gardener was near
her, but he seemed unaware of anyone but Alleyn and the
doctor. He looked from one to the other, distractedly
moving his head like someone in pain. When he saw Nigel
he walked over to him swiftly and stood beside him. Nigel
took hold of his arm and squeezed it. In the wings,
masked in shadows, were groups of people.

" I haven't moved him," said the doctor. " It's a very
superficial examination, but quite enough for your purpose. He was shot through the heart and died instantly."

" I shot him," said Gardener suddenly. " I've killed him.
I've killed Arthur."

The doctor glanced at him uneasily.

" Shut up, Felix," Nigel murmured. He looked at Alleyn.
The inspector was standing talking to George Simpson.
They walked to the prompt box. Simpson was showing
Alleyn something. It was the gun he used for the faked
report.

" I never knew," he kept saying. " They went off at the
same time. I never knew. This was a blank. I never even
pointed it. It couldn't have done anything, could it?"

Alleyn came back on to the stage. He spoke to all the
people in the wings on the set. " Will you all go to
the wardrobe-room, please? I shall take statements later.
You will, of course, want to change and take off your war
paint. I am afraid I must forbid any access to the

34

dressing-rooms until I have been through them, but I understand there is a wash-basin and a mirror in the wardrobe-room and I shall have your things sent in to you there. Just a moment, please. Don't go yet."

Six men were making their way through the crowd in the wings. Three of the newcomers were uniformed constables. The others were plain clothes men. They were given place and walked on to the stage.

"Well, Bailey," said Alleyn.

"Well, sir," said one of the plain clothes men. "What's the trouble?"

"As you see." Alleyn turned towards the body. The men pulled off their hats. One of them put a handbag down by Alleyn, who nodded. Detective-Sergeant Bailey, a finger-print official, bent down and looked at the body.

"You men," said Alleyn to the constables, "take everyone to the wardrobe-room. One of you stay outside and one at the stage door. Nobody to come out or go in. Mr. Simpson will show you. He goes in too. Please, Mr. Simpson."

The stage manager started forward and looked wanly round the stage.

"Everybody in the wardrobe-room, please," he said, as though he was calling a rehearsal. He turned to the constables. "This way, please," he added.

He walked off the stage, a policeman following him. A second man waited a moment and then said:

"Just move along, please, ladies and gentlemen." Old Susan Max, roundabout, sensible, said: "Come along, dear," to Miss Vaughan. Miss Vaughan stretched out her hands dumbly to Gardener, who did not look at her. She turned towards Alleyn, who watched her curiously, and then, with a very touching dignity, she let herself be led off by Susan Max. At the doorway she turned and looked again at the dead man, shuddered, and disappeared into the wings.

"Lovely exit, wasn't it?" said the inspector.

"Alleyn!" exclaimed Nigel, really shocked.

Miss Janet Emerald the "heavy" woman, said: "Bounder!" from behind a piece of scenery.

"Let us go," replied the voice of J. Barclay Crammer. "We are in these people's hands." He appeared on the stage, crossed it, and gripped Gardener's hand. "Come, old man," he said. "With me. Together."

"Oh, get along, the whole lot of you," exclaimed Alleyn with the utmost impatience. Mr. Crammer looked at him, more in sorrow than in anger, and did as he suggested. Gardener straightened his back and managed the veriest ghost of a smile. "You agree with me about actors, I see," he said.

Alleyn responded instantly: "They are a bit thick, aren't they?"

"I want to say," said Gardener, "that I know I've killed him; but, before God, Mr. Alleyn, I didn't load that revolver."

"Don't talk," said Nigel. "They'll find out everything—they'll clear you. Don't worry more than you can help, you know."

Gardener waited a moment. He looked like a man coming round from concussion to realise gradually his abominable surroundings.

"Look here," he said suddenly. "Somebody must have——" He stopped short. A terrified look came into his eyes. Nigel took him by the elbow again and gently urged him forward. "You're a decent old sausage, Nigel," he said uncertainly. "Oh, well——"

"Now!" said Alleyn with relief.

They all turned to him.

"Can we have the whole story?" asked the older of the two C.I.D. men.

"You can. Here it is——"

Alleyn was interrupted by a shrill scream that seemed to come from the dressing-room passage. A woman's voice raised in hideous falsetto was mingled with an exasperated baritone. "Let me alone, let me alone, let me alone!"

"Oh, Lord, more highstrikes!" said Chief Detective-Inspector Alleyn. "Go and see what it's about, Bailey."

Detective-Sergeant Bailey did as he was told. His voice,

a deep bass, soon mingled reasonably in the uproar : " Now, then, now then, this won't do;" and then the constable :

" Only obeying orders, miss."

The noise grew fainter. A door slammed. Bailey reappeared, looking scandalised. " One of the ladies, sir," he said. " Trying to get into her room."

" Did she get in?" asked Alleyn sharply.

" Well, yes, she did for a minute. Kind of slipped away from the rest of the mob before the P.C. could stop her. He yanked her out of it, quick time."

" Who was it?"

" I think the name was Emerald," said Bailey disgustedly. " Surname, I mean," he added quickly.

" What did she do it for?"

" Something about getting something for her face, she said, sir."

" Well, she's stowed away with the others now," commented Alleyn grimly. " Sit down, all of you. Bathgate, stay if you like, and you too, Dr. Milner."

" Shall I wait?" asked the business manager.

" Yes, if you will, Mr. Stavely. I may want you." They all sat in the heavy leather chairs, and Nigel thought they looked as if they were arranging themselves for the curtain to go up.

" The situation, briefly, is this," Alleyn began. " The body is that of Mr. Arthur Surbonadier. During the course of the last act he played a scene with Mr. Gardener and Miss Vaughan. He threatened Gardener with that revolver lying there. Miss Vaughan covered him from the doorway. Gardener took the revolver from him. He made as if he would strangle Gardener, who raised the gun and shot him at close quarters. The gun business has always been faked. The report comes from the wings. A blank was never used on the stage, as it would have scorched Surbonadier's clothes. There's no doubt where the shot came from. To-night the revolver was loaded, and not with ' dummies.' Let's have a photo of the body, and one of the stage."

One of the plain clothes men went into the stage door

passage and returned with a camera. Several photos were taken. The camera-man, a completely silent individual, then removed himself and his paraphernalia.

"This is our divisional surgeon, Dr. Milner."

"Good evening," said the two medicos simultaneously. The divisional surgeon made a brief examination of the body and stood apart talking to Dr. Milner.

"Run a chalk round the body, Bailey, and turn it over," said Alleyn.

Bailey knelt down and did this. Surbonadier was lying half on his face. When he was turned over Nigel forced himself to look at him. He had the same astonished expression as they had seen from their place in the stalls. The grease paint shone dully on the dead face. The eyes were wide open.

"You notice the scorched clothes. He was killed instantly.

"Shot through the heart," said the doctor.

"God, it's awful!" said the manager suddenly.

"I think that will do." Alleyn turned to the divisional surgeon, who knelt beside Surbonadier and closed the painted eyelids. Bailey, who had just gone off the stage for a moment, reappeared with a length of brocade, with which he covered the body. It was a flamboyant thing, flame-coloured and gold.

"The revolver will, of course, show Mr. Gardener's prints," Alleyn said. "But you will test it for others, please, Bailey. It was in his dressing-room at seven-twenty, when I saw it." Bailey glanced at him in surprise. "The dresser took it to Mr. Surbonadier some time between seven-thirty and seven forty-five. It was then unloaded and Surbonadier himself loaded it on the stage. We must remember that everyone in the cast knew exactly what would happen. Mr. Gardener was certain to do precisely what he did do—press the barrel of the revolver into Surbonadier above the heart and pull the trigger. There may be a remote possibility that Surbonadier was accidentally supplied with genuine ammunition. It seems scarcely likely. If he was deliberately supplied with live cartridges, the person responsible would be tolerably certain of results. Surbonadier was scarcely off the stage after he loaded the gun, and while on the stage would not fire, since even an unloaded revolver makes a loud click if this is done. Gardener would be certain to pull the trigger. His hand was in full view of the audience and the illusion had to be complete. Am I right, Mr. Stavely?"

"Yes. Yes, I think so, but, you know, the production is not my province, inspector. I belong to the front of the house. The producer is in Manchester, but Mr. Simpson, the general manager, would be your best authority—or Gardener himself."

"Of course, yes. Will you be kind enough to get Mr. Simpson for me? Oh—and, Mr. Stavely, take Detective-Sergeant Bailey with you and show him the dressing-rooms. Bailey, don't disturb any room but Miss Max's. From that you may take a towel and soap and a pot of grease. They take their paint off with grease, don't they? Take the stuff to the wardrobe-room, then lock the dressing-room doors and let 'em wash. And, Fox"—he turned to the second plain clothes man—"be a saint and ring for the mortuary van. Mr. Stavely will take you to the telephone. Sorry to be a bit Hitlerish, but it'll save time." He smiled charmingly at Stavely and the doctor. "Thank you very much, Dr. Milner. I shan't bother you any more to-night, but I've got your address. I'm sure you're longing to get way."

The doctor looked very much as though he was longing to stay. However, he departed meekly, escorted by the divisional surgeon. The others went on their errands and Nigel was left alone with Alleyn.

The theatre had become very silent. Far away in the front of the house a door slammed and immediately afterwards they heard a clock strike. Eleven. Twenty minutes ago the dead man under the length of brocade had been vigorous and alert; the echo of his voice had scarcely died away. To Nigel it seemed more like two hours.

"Alleyn," he said suddenly, "you don't think it was Felix, do you?"

"Bless the boy, I'm not a medium. I haven't the foggiest idea who it was, but he's no likelier than any of the others. He didn't load the revolver. The fact of his pulling the trigger doesn't appear to be particularly relevant. I say it doesn't *appear* to be. He may have to answer a technical charge of manslaughter. I don't know. Don't understand law."

"Bosh."

"Don't say bosh to me, child. Can you write shorthand?"

"Yes."

"Then take this note-book, sit on the other side of the scenery, and write down the ensuing conversations. Do it quietly. Your finger on your lips and all that."

"I don't want your note-book. Got one of my own."

"As you please. Here comes Simpson. Skedaddle." Nigel slipped out of the upstage entrance, leaving the door ajar. In the half-light offstage he saw a large round footstool of the type know as a "pouf." He pulled it quietly towards the entrance, sat down, and took out his scribbling pad and stylo. He heard someone come down the dressing-room passage and walk on to the stage at the prompt corner. From behind the scene flat, and quite close to him, Alleyn spoke.

"Oh, here you are, Mr. Simpson. Frightfully sorry to keep you all hanging about like this, but I want to do as much as I can before the scent, if there is a scent, grows cold. Do sit down."

There was a gentle sound of a soft impact, and the rustle of a silk cushion. Then Simpson spoke. "Of course—anything I can do to help."

"I want you to tell me 'in your own words,' as leading counsel loves to say, the exact procedure that took place every evening, and particularly this evening, in regard to the ammunition used in the revolver. As I remember,, Mr. Surbonadier loaded the revolver with cartridges that he took from a drawer in a writing-desk during the first scene in the last act. Who put those cartridges there?"

"The murderer."

"I see," said Alleyn good-humouredly, "that you take my point. I should have said : Who put the dummy cartridges there?"

"I did," said George Simpson.

Chapter V

STATEMENT OF THE STAGE MANAGER

Nigel experienced a slight thrill in taking down Simpson's last statement—a thrill that was at once tempered by the reflection that the placing of the dummy cartridges was of little importance in tracing the deadly ones. Alleyn went on easily :

"You did. Splendid. Now, when exactly did you put the dummies in that drawer?"

"During the second act wait, just before the curtain went up."

"The desk was then on the stage, or should I say on the set?"

"Only if you're a talkie actor. The scene was set and the desk was in position."

"I wish there had been no further change of scene. Where exactly was the desk? As I remember, it was about here."

Nigel heard Alleyn walk across the stage. By dint of squinting through the crack in the doorway he saw that the inspector was standing in the prompt first entrance, that is to say, in the doorway on the audience's right of the stage.

"It was just upstage of there," said Simpson.

"And the face of the desk towards the door, wasn't it?" asked Alleyn.

"That is so."

41

"Now, when you put the dummies in the drawer who was on the stage?"

"The beginners for the third act. Miss Max, Miss Emerald, and—Mr. Surbonadier."

"Did they see you put them there?"

"Oh, yes. Janet said : 'I'm always terrified you'll forget those things, George. You leave it so late!'"

"The drawer was empty when you pulled it out?"

"I think so. I don't know that I'd swear it was—I may not have looked at the back of it."

"Do you remember if any of the others afterwards came near the desk? Perhaps sat down at it while waiting for the curtain to go up?"

"I don't remember," said Simpson in a great hurry.

"Mr. Simpson—try to remember." There was a pause.

"I can't remember," said Simpson querulously.

"Let me try and help. Did you speak to any of them, now?"

"Yes. Yes, I did. I spoke to Miss Max, who was over on the O.P. She said the rug on that side was in the way of the door opening, and I moved it for her. Then she sat down in the chair over there and took out her knitting. The knitting is 'business' in the part."

"Yes. She had it in a red bag."

"That's right." Simpson began to speak very rapidly. "And she didn't move again before the curtain went up. I remember that because she laughed about her knitting and said she was trying to get it finished before we had run three weeks. It's a scarf. She put it round my neck to measure it."

"Now, didn't she sit in that chair for some time after the curtain went up? Wasn't she still sitting there when Surbonadier loaded the revolver?"

Through the crack in the door Nigel saw Simpson's surprised glance at the inspector.

"You've got a good memory," he said. "That's perfectly true."

"I've got a rotten memory really," said Alleyn, "but the scene impressed me, you know. If you think back it's a great help. Now, what did you do after you had straightened the mat and had your merry jape with the knitting?"

" I think I had a look round the stage to see everything was in place."

" And then——?"

" Then I went to the prompt box. I remember now that Surbonadier and Miss Emerald were standing upstage by the window and——" He stopped short.

" Yes?"

" That's all."

" I don't think so, Mr. Simpson. What were you going to say?"

" Nothing."

" I can't force you to speak, but do—do let me urge you to consider the seriousness of your position. It's no good my pretending or trying to bluff. I'm no actor, Mr. Simpson. You put the cartridges in the drawer. It's of first importance from your point of view to prove that they were dummy cartridges."

" It's not for myself——" began Simpson hotly.

" Then don't for the love of Mike start some fool game of shielding another person. That sort of thing is either damn' dangerous or just plain silly. However, it's as you please."

Simpson moved away from the range of Nigel's vision and when he did speak his voice sounded remote.

" You're quite right, I suppose," he said. " As for myself, I think I can clear up the cartridge business."

" All to the good. Now what were you going to say about Miss Janet Emerald?"

" Honestly, it's nothing really. Arthur Surbonadier semed a bit upset. He—well, it's my job as stage manager to look after that sort of thing—he was not himself."

" You mean he was drunk—I know he was."

" Oh—well—yes, that and something else. Sort of dangerous drunk. Well, when I went back to the prompt box Janet Emerald came after me and she said : 'Arthur's tight, George, and I'm nervous,' and I said : 'He's giving a damn' good show, anyway.' (He was, you know.) Then she said : 'That may be right, but he's a beast, a

43

filthy beast.' And I heard her whisper—— Oh, lord, it meant nothing——"

" Well?"

" She whispered to herself : ' I could kill him '; and then she turned her back to me and stood with her hands on the desk. She talks that way. It meant nothing. I didn't look at her again. I glanced at the book and said : ' All clear, please,' and they took up positions."

" And then?"

" Then I said : ' House lights ' to the switchboard man and flicked on the orchestra warning and the black-out warning. That scene opens on a black-out."

" Yes."

" Well, then I said : ' Stand by, please,' and we blacked out and the scene went up."

" How long did the black-out last?"

" For the first few speeches of the dialogue. About four minutes altogether, because we black out for a little before the curtain goes up. Then Surbonadier switched on the stage lamp."

" Who was on the stage, behind the scenes, all that time?"

" Oh, the staff were up at the back. The property master and others. Props was standing beside me in the prompt box, I remember. He stayed there after he had given me the dummies and was there all the time until after the black-out. I know that because he kept whispering something about one of the dummies being loose. He seemed scared it might come to bits when Surbonadier loaded the gun."

" I see. And the others?"

" I think young Howard Melville was somewhere round —he's assistant S.M. I was on the book. It's a short scene, but the beginners in the next bit aren't called until half-way through."

" One more point and then I'm done. Where did you get the dummies?"

" Props made them. He's a positive genius at anything like that. Takes a pride in it. He got empty shells and filled them with sand, and then shoved the bullets in."

"Rather unnecessarily thorough, one would think."

"Lord, yes!" Simpson sounded much more at ease now. "But that's Props all over. He was shell-shocked during the war, poor devil, and he's—not exactly queer—but kind of intensely concentrated. He was as proud as Punch when he showed them to me, and said no one could tell they weren't the goods."

"Where were they kept?"

"Props always picked up the revolver at the end of the show and took them out. Then he used to take the gun to Felix Gardener. It was his brother's gun and Felix sets great store by it and always takes it home. Props used to put the dummies into the property-room and bring them to me before that scene. I made him do that because I wanted to be quite certain they were in the right drawer."

"And that's what happened to-night?"

"Yes."

"Did you examine them before you put them in the drawer?"

"I don't think so—I—I don't know."

"Would you have known if they were genuine ammunition?"

"I don't know—yes, I'm sure I would."

"In spite of the property master's art?"

"I don't know, I tell you."

"All right, all right, keep your hair on. If the property man was worried about the loose cartridge——"

"Yes. Yes, of course. They must have been dummies."

"Q.E.D. Now, Mr. Simpson, that's all for the moment. I see Inspector Fox is waiting out there. Just give him your address, will you, and get him to take you to your dressing-room? Show him which clothes you want to change into—no, wait a second; you're in a dinner jacket, and I imagine won't need to change. Fox!"

"Hullo!"

"Has the van come."

"Outside now."

"Oh. Well, see if Mr. Simpson wants anything from his dressing-room. And, Mr. Simpson, will you let Inspec-

45

tor Fox just have a look at you? Pure formality and
whatnot. You needn't if you want to. Don't get all
het up over it."

Simpson's reply to this speech was indistinguishable.
Nigel, by dint of widening his peephole, could see Fox
going rapidly and thoroughly through the stage manager's
pockets.

"Cigarette-case, two pounds in notes and cash, pocket-
book, handkerchief, matches, no written matter at all.
Want to see anything, sir?" he asked cheerfully.

"Not a thing. One last question. Would Gardener be
certain to pull the trigger when he pretended to fire the
shot into the Beaver?"

"Definitely certain. It was rehearsed most carefully.
He always closed his left hand a fraction of a second
before he pulled the trigger. That gave me the cue for
the blank shot."

"I see, yes. Thank you so much. Good night, Mr.
Simpson."

Fox and the stage manager walked away. Nigel was
wondering if he might speak when Alleyn's face suddenly
appeared close to the door. The inspector laid his finger
on his nose and made a face at Nigel, who was rather
shocked at this display. Alleyn opened the door and
came out. Nigel saw men with a stretcher on the stage
and suddenly shut the door to. Alleyn looked curiously,
but not unsympathetically, at him.

"Exit an actor, eh?" he said.

"You're a callous old pig," said Nigel.

"Did you get all that down?"

"I did."

"Good boy. Hullo, who's this? Stay where you are
and stand by."

Voices, noisy in argument, could be heard from somewhere near the stage door.

"What the hell d'yer mean?" someone inquired loudly.
"It's my theatre. Get out of my light."

Nigel returned to his peephole. The body of Surbonadier
had gone. Inspector Fox appeared in hot pursuit of a
monster of a man in tails, with a gardenia in his coat. He

advanced truculently upon Alleyn, uttering a sort of roaring noise.

"Mr. Jacob Saint, I believe," said the inspector politely.

"And who the devil are you?"

"From the Yard, Mr. Saint, and in charge of this unhappy business. I am sorry you should have to meet such shocking news—I see you have heard of the tragedy. Mr. Surbonadier was your nephew, wasn't he? May I offer my sympathy?"

"Who's the swine that did him in?"

"At present we don't know."

"Was he drunk?"

"Since you ask me—yes."

Jacob Saint eyed the inspector and suddenly threw his bulk into an arm-chair. Nigel was seized with an idea and began taking notes again.

"I was in front to-night," said Saint.

"I saw you," said Alleyn brightly.

"I didn't know he was dead, but I knew he was drunk. He did it himself."

"You think so?" Alleyn seemed quite unmoved by this announcement.

"Stavely rang me up at the Savoy. I was behind, earlier in the evening, and saw Arthur. He was tight then. I told him he'd have to get out at the end of the week. Couldn't face the music and killed himself."

"It would take extraordinary fortitude to load a revolver, play a part, and wait for another man to shoot you, I should have thought," remarked Alleyn mildly.

"He was drunk."

"So we agreed. He had provided himself with live cartridges before he was drunk perhaps."

"What d'yer mean? Oh. Wouldn't put it past him. Where's Janet?"

"Who?"

"Miss Emerald."

"The artists are all in the wardrobe-room."

"I'll go and see her."

"Please don't move, Mr. Saint. I'll let her know. Miss Emerald, please, Fox."

47

Inspector Fox went. Saint glared after him, appeared to hesitate and then produced a cigar-case. "Smoke?" he said.

"No, thank you so much," said Alleyn. "I'm for a pipe."

Saint lit a cigar.

"Understand this," he said. "I'm no hypocrite and I don't spill any sob stuff over Arthur. He was a rotten failure. When one of my shows crashes I forget about it —a dud speculation. So was Arthur. Rotten all through, and a coward, but enough of an actor to see himself in a star part at last—and play it. He was crazy to play a big part, and when I wouldn't give him 'Carruthers' he— he actually threatened me—me!"

"Where did you see him to-night?"

"In his dressing-room. I had business in the office here and went behind."

"Would you care to tell me what happened?"

"Told you already. He was drunk and I fired him."

"What did he say?"

"Didn't wait to listen. I had an appointment in the office for seven-fifteen. Janet!" Saint's voice changed. He got to his feet. Nigel moved a little and saw that Janet Emerald had appeared in the prompt doorway. She gave a loud cry, rushed across the stage and threw herself into Saint's arms.

"Jacco! Jacco!" she sobbed.

"Poor baby—poor baby," Saint murmured, and Nigel marvelled at the kindness in his voice as he soothed the somewhat large and overwhelming Miss Emerald.

"It wasn't you," she said suddenly. "They can't say it was you!" She threw her head back distractedly and her face, cleaned now of its make-up, looked ghastly. Saint had his back to Nigel, but it was sufficiently eloquent of the shock her words had given him. Still holding her, he was frozen into immobility. When he spoke his voice was controlled but no longer tender.

"Poor kid," he said, in the best theatre-magnate manner. "You're all hysterical. Me! Do I seem like a murderer, baby?"

48

"No. no—I'm mad. It was so awful, Jacco. Jacco, it was so awful."

"M-m—m-m—m-m," growled Mr. Saint soothingly.

"Quite." Alleyn's voice cut in. "Most unpleasant. I am sure you must be longing to get away from it all, Miss Emerald."

"I'll drive you home," offered Jacob Saint. He and Miss Emerald stood side by side now and Nigel could see how pale they both were.

"An excellent idea." Alleyn's voice sounded close to the door. "But first of all may I just put a few questions to Miss Emerald?"

"You may not," said Saint. "If you want anything you can come and see her to-morrow. Get that?"

"Oh, yes, rather. Full in the teeth. Afraid, however, it makes no difference. There's a murder charge hovering round waiting for somebody, Mr. Saint, and shall we say a drama is being produced which you do not control and in which you play a part that may or may not be significant? To carry my flight of fancy a bit farther, I may add that the flat-footed old Law is stage manager, producer, and critic. And I, Mr. Saint, in the words of an old box-office success, 'I, my Lords, embody the law.' Sit down if you want to and please keep quiet. Now then, Miss Emerald."

Chapter VI

INTO THE SMALL HOURS

Nigel took down every word of Alleyn's little speech with the liveliest enthusiasm. At the conclusion he wrote in brackets: "Noise of theatre magnate sitting down." In a moment he was busy again. Alleyn had concentrated on Miss Janet Emerald.

"Do you mind if I light my pipe, Miss Emerald? Thank

you. Oh—cigarette? Those are Turks and those are—but I expect you know that one."

"No, thank you."

A match scraped, and Alleyn spoke between sucks at his pipe.

"Well, now. Will you tell me, as far as you know, how the business of loading the revolver was managed?" ("But he knows all that," thought Nigel impatiently.)

"I—I know nothing about it—I had nothing to do with it," said Janet Emerald.

"Of course not. But perhaps you noticed who put the blank cartridges in the drawer, and when."

"I didn't notice at all—anything about the cartridges."

"Did you never see them put in the drawer?"

"I didn't notice."

"Really? You didn't concern yourself about whether they were there, or say to Mr. Simpson that you were terrified he would forget them?"

"I couldn't have done so. What makes you think I said anything of the sort? Jacco! I don't know what I'm saying. Please—please, can't I go?"

"Don't move, Mr. Saint, I shall soon be done. Now, Miss Emerald, please answer my questions as best you can and as simply as you can. Believe me, an innocent person has nothing to fear and everything to gain in telling the truth. You are not the silly, bewildered little thing you pretend to be. You are a large and, I should say, very intelligent woman."

"Jacco!"

"And I suggest that you behave like one. Now, please—did you or did you not notice Mr. Simpson placing the cartridges to-night, and did you, or did you not, remark that you were afraid he'd forget to do so?"

"No, no, no—it's all a lie."

"And did you afterwards go and stand with your hands on the desk?"

"Never—I was talking to Arthur—I didn't notice what George Simpson was doing—he's telling lies. If that's what he says, he's lying."

"What were you saying to Mr. Surbonadier? It must

50

have been of some interest to absorb all your attention."

" I don't remember."

" Really?"

" I don't remember. I don't remember."

" Thank you. Fox, ask Miss Susan Max if she'll be good
enough to come here."

" That mean we can go?" Saint's voice made Nigel
jump—he had forgotten the proprietor of the Unicorn.

" In a minute. The night is young. How impatient you
are, to be sure."

" What sort of a breed are you?" asked Saint suddenly.
" Gentleman 'tec, or the comedian of the Yard, or what?"

" My dear Mr. Saint, you make me feel quite shy."

" Ow yow—yow—yow," Saint echoed the inspector's
pleasant voice with the exasperated facetiousness of a
street urchin. " All Oxford and Cambridge and hot air,"
he added savagely.

" Only Oxford, and that's nothing nowadays," said
Alleyn apologetically. " Oh, here you are, Miss Max." His
voice was cordial, " I can't tell you how bad I feel about
giving you all this trouble," Miss Max had waddled into
Nigel's line of sight.

" Never you mind," she said comfortably. " You're only
doing your job, I suppose."

" Miss Max, if only everyone felt like that a policeman's
lot would be a happier one."

" I played Ruth in *Pirates* on the Australian circuit,"
said Miss Max, letting herself down into the chair the
inspector had pushed forward.

" Did you really? Do you remember the trio about the
paradox? Frederick, Ruth, and Pirate King?"

" Indeed I do.

"A paradox,
A paradox,
A most ingenious paradox,"

sang Miss Max in a jolly wheeze.

" Susan!" wailed Miss Emerald. " How can you?"

" Why not, dear? It's a lovely number."

" There's something of a paradox here," said Alleyn,
" that you can solve for us."

"And you're the policeman."

"Yes—would you call me 'Frederick' and may I call you 'Ruth'?"

"Get along with you!" said old Susan Max.

"Well, here it is. Perhaps I won't tell you the paradox but ask you a question and hope that your answer will explain it. Can you tell me just what happened on the stage before the curtain went up on the last act?"

"Susan," began Janet Emerald. "You remember——"

"Please!" (Alleyn made Nigel jump.) "Now, Miss Max."

"Well, let me think. I was sitting on the O.P. knitting my scarf and scolding George Simpson about that mat. 'George,' I said, 'do you want me to break my neck?' So he fixed it. Little things like that look so bad from the front, and it quite spoilt my eggzit at the end of that scene."

"I enjoyed your reading of the part enormously."

"Well, dear, I made it a type, you know."

"Is this a cosy chat or a statement?" inquired Saint.

"It's a dialogue between two people only," answered Alleyn. "It's a great thing to be able to study types, Miss Max—I have to do a bit of that myself."

"It's all observation," said Miss Max in a gratified tone.

"Of course it is. You've learnt to observe. You can be of the greatest help to me. Now, can you tell me, Miss Max, exactly what happened after Mr. Simpson put the mat straight?"

"Now, let me think," said Susan Max. There was a dead silence. Miss Emerald gave a sob.

"Yes," said Susan suddenly. "Janet was upset and talking to poor Arthur, who was a little pizzicato."

"Pizzicato?"

"A little too much wine taken. Pity. Well, they whispered together and then he said to her——No. I'm telling stories. *She* said to *him*: 'Are you all right?'; and *he* said to *her*: 'No, I'm all blanky wrong,' using language as he did so. I didn't hear the next bit, but presently he said in an extremely disagreeable manner; 'You can't talk about influence, Janet. You wouldn't be where you are without it.' More whispers. I didn't listen. I measured my scarf round George Simpson's neck. Then when he went off to the prompt corner—— No, I've left out a bit. Wait, *Before* that, when George put the cartridges in the drawer, Janet said she was always afraid he'd forget them —do you remember, dear? And then *after* all the other bit about poor Arthur being drunk and influence and so forth, you followed over to the prompt corner and I recollect that you had another whisper with him—with George Simpson, I mean, of course. There you are!" Miss Max ended with a sort of triumphant gaiety.

"Bravo!" cried Alleyn. "Top marks. We shall have to get you into the force."

"Oh, yes, I dare say. Well, now. Is that all? Can I go?"

"I shall be sorry to lose you."

Nigel had waited for an outburst from Miss Emerald— a denial, an explanation, another bout of hysteria. Instead there was a dead silence. He wished he could see Janet Emerald and Jacob Saint.

"It's a shocking thing," said Susan Max abruptly. 'It's a very shocking thing for a young man to die as Arthur Surbonadier died. Not himself. Angry. For he *was* angry, you know."

"What about?"

"All sorts of things. Not satisfied with the casting. Unhappy over other matters too, I believe. I suppose it's murder?"

"It looks like it."

"And poor Felix. You're not running away with the idea Felix had anything to do with it, I hope? Except pulling the trigger, poor fellow. Um?"

"Why not?" Janet Emerald demanded. "Why not Felix Gardener? He shot him. It was his revolver. Why is everybody so sure he knew nothing about it? Stephanie doing brave heroine stuff all over him. Everybody treating him like an invalid. While I—I—am treated like a criminal. It's infamous."

"There's only one thing more," said Alleyn, exactly as if she had not spoken. "It's unavoidable or I wouldn't press it. I should like everyone behind the scenes to-night to be searched before they leave. I can't insist, but it will save a lot of bother if you consent. Miss Max, I expect you know what we are looking for?"

"I don't, then."

"For the dummy cartridges."

"Oh."

"They will be fairly bulky. Miss Emerald, will you take off your wrap?"

"Here!" said Jacob Saint. "Whaddeyer going to do?"

"Oh, hold your tongue, Jacco!"

A slithery noise. Nigel craned his neck and saw Janet Emerald move forward. She was clad in a sequinned sheath that fitted her like a skin.

"Miss Emerald, will you let me make a very superficial examination or would you prefer to go to a police station, where there will be a wardress?"

"Don't let him touch you, Janet."

"Oh, Jacco, don't be a fool." There was no touch of hysteria here, only a harsh and wearied contempt. "Do whatever you like," said Janet Emerald. She held up her magnificent arms and closed her eyes. Alleyn passed his delicate hands lightly over the surface of her dress. He too had closed his eyes. He looked as though his brain was in his fingertips. There was something uncannily remote about him. Lightly the hands swept down the sides and front of the sequinned dress, down the flanks, pausing at the knees and then dropping disinterestedly away. He picked up the fallen wrap, felt it all over, shook it and held it out politely by the collar. "You would like to put it on again," he said.

Janet Emerald breathed unevenly and a curious, distorted smile visited her lips. She slid into the wrap.

"And what about you, Miss Max?" said Alleyn.

"I'm more bulky—you'll have to prod," said Susan Max cheerfully. She took off her overcoat and stood, a round, and somehow pathetic, figure in blouse and skirt.

"You are very courteous," said Alleyn gravely. "And very wise."

He searched her and then Jacob Saint, who stood up

for it without protest or comment. Alleyn looked carefully at the papers in his pocket-book, but appeared to find nothing that interested him.

"That is all," he said at last. "I'll keep you no longer. How will you get home, Miss Max?"

"I live in South Kensington—I suppose I've missed the last bus."

"Fox. Be a good fellow and tell the constable at the door to get a taxi. My party, Miss Max."

"You *are* kind," said Susan Max.

"Good night—'Ruth.' Good night, Miss Emerald. Mr. Saint. Inspector Fox will take your addresses."

"Here!" said Saint suddenly. "Maybe I've been short with you, inspector. This thing's upset me. You're doing your duty and I respect that. I'd like to see you to-morrow."

"I shall be at the Yard at eleven, should you wish to make a statement, Mr. Saint."

"Statement be damned."

"By all means. Good night."

Footsteps and then silence.

"Still awake, Bathgate?" asked Alleyn.

"Just," said Nigel. "Let me come out there for a minute. I'm all pins and needles."

"Come out, come out, my dearest dear. What did you think of little Janet? And Uncle Jacob?"

"Not much." Nigel emerged and stood blinking. "By Jove, she told some stinking big whoppers."

"She did rather."

"I say—do you think——"

"Only very confusedly. It's all so muddly."

"I distrust you intensely," said Nigel, "when you go on like that."

"Get back to your corner. Who shall we have next?"

"Don't ask me. It's beastly cold on this stage."

"Shall we adjourn to a dressing-room?"

"Good idea—whose?"

"Bailey has been searching them while you were in your cosy corner. I rather fancy Arthur Surbonadier's."

55

" You old ghoul. May I ask if you intend to search all the ladies?"

" Don't you think it quate nayce?"

" No, I don't."

" P'r'aps you're right. Hullo, Bailey."

The fingerprint expert reappeared.

" I've been through the rooms," he said in a bored voice. " No sign of the blanks. Got all their prints."

" Really—how?"

" Oh, asked for them." Bailey grinned sardonically. " You weren't there, sir."

" That's all right." Alleyn disliked asking directly for fingerprints and preferred to pick them up without the owner's knowledge. " Well," he said, " We'd better get on with the good work."

" We could do with those dummies," Bailey remarked. " Inspector Fox is searching the other men now, sir. Thought it would save you the trouble."

" Intelligent as well as kind. But he won't find them."

" The dummies?" Bailey eyed his surprise.

" The dummies. Unless our murderer is particularly vindictive."

" What's this?" demanded Nigel suspiciously. " Isn't a murderer usually rather vindictive?"

" You don't understand, I'm afraid," said Alleyn kindly. " I think—" he added, turning to Bailey—" I think the cartridges will be in the obvious place."

" Obvious!" repeated Bailey. " You've got me beat, sir? Is there an obvious place?"

" You'll never make a murderer, Bailey. Before we move away let us have a look at that desk. It's in the wings, there. Give me a hand."

Nigel stood near the centre of the stage. He had moved forward towards the wings, when a voice, raucous and detached, yelled above their heads.

" Look out!"

An instant later, Inspector Alleyn hurled himself full at Nigel, driving him backwards. He fell sprawling across a chair, and at the same moment was aware of something else that fell from above, and crashed down deafeningly on to the stage. Something that raised a cloud of dust.

He got to his feet shaken and bewildered. Lying on the stage was a shattered heap of broken glass. Alleyn stood near it, looking up into the flies.

" Come down out of that," he shouted.

" Yessir. Coming, sir."

" Who the devil are you?" bawled Bailey suddenly.

" Only the props, sir. I'm coming."

They stumbled into the wings, where they were all met by Inspector Fox who had run agitatedly from the wardrobe-room. They all peered up the wall of the stage. An iron ladder ran aloft into the shadows. Soft footsteps padded up there in the dark, and presently among the shadows a darker shape could be seen. The iron ladder vibrated very faintly. Somebody was coming down.

Chapter VII

PROPS

The shadowy figure came very deliberately down the ladder. Nigel, Alleyn and Bailey did not speak, but fell back a little. Nigel was still shaken by his escape from the chandelier. He felt bewildered, and watched, without thinking, the rubber soles of a pair of dilapidated tennis shoes come down, rung by rung. The man did not turn his face away from the wall until he had completed his descent. Then he swung round slowly.

Bailey moved forward and seized his arm.

" Now then—you," he said.

" Don't you act old-fashioned at me," snarled the man.

" Just a minute, Bailey," said Alleyn. Bailey stared indignantly round.

" You're the property master," said Alleyn. The man stood with his heels together and his hands held tidily at the seams of his trousers. His face was long, thin, and white; with eyebrows that grew together. He looked fixedly at a spot on the scenery above the inspector's head.

"Yessir," he said.

"Been at this job long?"

"Ever since I was demobbed."

"In the Brigade of Guards, weren't you?"

"Yessir. Grenadiers, sir. King's Company."

"You made the dummy cartridges for this show?"

"Yessir."

"Where are they?"

"I gave them to Mr. Simpson."

"The dummy cartridges. Are you sure of that?"

"Yessir."

"How are you so sure? They might have been the real thing."

"No, sir." The man swallowed. "I was looking at them. I dropped a cartridge, and the bullet was loose, sir."

"Where are they now?"

"I dunno, sir."

"How did you come to drop that chandelier?"

Silence.

"How is it fixed up there?"

"On a pulley."

"And the rope turned round a piece of wood or something, to make it fast?"

"Yessir."

"Did the rope break or did you unwind it?"

"I can't say, sir."

"Very well. Sergeant Bailey, go up and have a look at the rope there, will you? Now, Props, you go up to the switch-board and give us some light behind the scenes."

Props turned smartly and did as he was told. In a moment, light flooded the back-stage harshly while, with the facial expression popularly attributed to a boot, Bailey climbed the ladder.

"Now come back." Props returned.

Alleyn had moved over to the desk which stood a little way out from the wings. Nigel, Fox, and the property master followed him. He drew out a pocket-knife and slipped the front of the blade under the top left-hand drawer and pulled it out.

"That's where Surbonadier got the cartridges," he said. "It's empty. Bailey had better get to work on it, but he'll only find stage hands' prints and Surbonadier's, I expect. Now then."

Using the very greatest care to avoid touching the surface, Alleyn next drew out the second drawer with the point of his blade.

"And here we are," he said brightly.

The others bent forward. Lying in the drawer were six cartridges.

"By gum," said Fox, "you've got 'em."

With one accord he and Nigel turned to look at the property master. He was standing in his ridiculous posture of attention, staring, as usual, above their heads. Alleyn, still bent over the drawer, addressed him mildly.

"Look into that drawer. Don't touch anything. Are those the dummies you made?"

Props craned his long neck and bent forward stiffly.

"Well?"

"Yessir."

"Yes. And there—look—is the loose one. There is a grain or two of sand fallen out. You made a job of them. Why didn't you want me to find them?"

Props gave another exhibition of masterly silence.

"You bore me," said Alleyn. "And you behave oddly, and rather like an ass. You knew those dummies were in the drawer; you heard me say I was going to look for them. You were listening up there in the dark. So you cheerfully dropped half a ton of candelabrum on the stage, first warning us of its arrival, as apparently you weren't keen on staging another murder to-night. I suppose you hoped for a scene of general confusion, during which you would shin down the ladder and remove the dummies. It was a ridiculous manœuvre. The obvious inference is that you dumped the darn' things there yourself, and took to the rigging when the murder came off."

"That's right, sir," said Props surprisingly. "It looks that way, but I never."

59

"You are, as I have said, an ass; and I'm not sure I oughtn't to arrest you as a something-or-other after the fact."

"My Gawd, I never done it, sir!"

"I'm delighted to hear you say so. Why, then, should you wish to shield the murderer? Oh, well, if you won't answer me, you won't; and I refuse to go on giving an imitation of a gentleman talking to himself. I shall have to detain you in a police station, Props."

A kind of tremor seemed to shake the man. His arms twitched convulsively and his eyes widened. Nigel, who was not familiar with the after-effects of shell-shock, watched him with reluctant curiosity. Alleyn looked at him attentively.

"Well?" he said.

"I never done it," said Props in a breathless whisper. "I never done it. You don't want to lock me up. I was standing in the prompt box and if I thought I seen a bloke or it might have been a woman, moving round in the dark——" He stopped short.

"You'd much better say so," said Alleyn.

"I don't want to get nobody in for the job. He was a swine. Whoever done it, done no 'arm, to my way of thinking."

"You didn't care for Mr. Surbonadier?"

Props uttered a few well-chosen and highly illuminating words. "He was" were the only two of them that were printable.

"Why do you say that?" asked Alleyn. "Has he ever done you any harm?"

The man made as if to speak, hesitated, and then, to Nigel's horror and embarrassment, began to cry.

"Fox," said Alleyn, "will you and Mr. Bathgate muster the rest of the stage staff, one by one, in a dressing-room or somewhere, and see if you can get any information from them? You know what we want. Unless anything crops up, you can let them go home. I'll sing out when I've finished."

Nigel thankfully followed Inspector Fox down the dressing-room passage and, Fox having unlocked the door, into Felix Gardener's room. It seemed an age since they had sat there, listening to his friend's views on the characteristics of actors.

"Well, sir," said Inspector Fox, "I reckoned that's our man."

"Do you really think so? Poor devil!"

"He's just the type. Neurotic, highly-strung sort of bloke."

"But," objected Nigel, "his alibi is supported by the stage manager."

"Yes—but suppose the cartridges he gave to the stage manager were the real Mackay?"

"What about the loose shell and the sand? That was true enough."

"Might have been loose when he put them in that drawer earlier in the evening—long before the black-out. Looks pretty queer, you must admit, sir. He scuttles up there into the grid when we are rounding up everyone else, and then, when Chief Inspector Alleyn says he'll take a look in the desk, Master Props lets loose that glass affair, hoping to get down in the confusion and slip out the dummies."

"Yes, but that chandelier business was so darn' silly," protested Nigel, "and if he did the murder, he's by no means silly. And why plant the dummies there, and then take such a clumsy and suspicious way of trying to divert your attention?"

"We'll have to get you in the force, sir," said Inspector Fox good-humouredly. "But all the same I think he's our man. The chief will be getting something now, I don't doubt. Well, sir, I'll just get the rest of the staff along."

The observations made by the rest of the staff of the Unicorn were singularly uninteresting. They were all in the property-room at the time of the black-out, preparing to enjoy a game of poker. In the words of their head, one Mr. Bert Willings: "They didn't know nuffing abaht it." Questioned about Props, Mr. Willings said: "Props was a funny bloke, very jumpy-like, and kep' hisself to hisself."

" Married?" asked Inspector Fox.

No, Props was not married, but he kep' company with Trixie Beadle, Miss Vaughan's dresser, wot was ole Bill Beadle's daughter. Ole Bill Beadle was Mr. Gardener's dresser.

" Who dressed Mr. Surbonadier?"

Old Bill also, it appeared. At this juncture one of the underlings remarked, unexpectedly and dramatically :

" 'E 'ated 'im."

" Who hated who?"

" Ole Bill 'e 'ated Mr. Sirbonbadier. For why? Because Mr. Sirbonbadier 'e was a-mucking arahnd Trixie."

" Er—" said Mr. Willings uneasily.

Fox pricked up his ears. " And how did Props like— er—the deceased—paying attention to his girl?'

" 'E 'ated 'im, too."

" Did he now," said Fox.

There was a short silence. Mr. Willings looked at his boots, stood uncertainly on one leg, grinned, and ran out of information. He and his myrmidons were told they might go home, having first left their names and addresses. They departed. Fox almost rubbed his hands together.

" There you are!" he exclaimed. " Deceased was interfering with his girl. He's just the type to go off the deep end. I think before we go any further I'd better let the big noise know about this."

They returned to the wings. Neither Alleyn or Props were to be seen.

" Well now," remarked Inspector Fox. " Where's he gone popping off to, I wonder?"

" Here I am," said Alleyn's voice. Nigel and Fox started slightly and walked round the prompt wing.

Alleyn and Bailey were on their knees by the prompt box. Bailey was busy with an insufflator and the chief inspector seemed to be peering at the floor through a magnifying glass. Beside him, opened, was the bag they had brought him from the Yard. Nigel looked into it and saw a neat collection of objects, among which he distinguished magnifying glasses, tape, scissors, soap, a towel, an electric torch, rubber gloves, sealing wax, and a pair of handcuffs.

" What are you doing?" asked Nigel.

" Being a detective. Can't you see?"

" What are you looking for?"

" Little signs of footprints, little grains of sand. Fox, my valued old one, my little brush is not in my case. Wing your way to Miss Vaughan's dressing-room and get the foot of my grandmother's hare which you will find on the dressing-table. Fetch me that foot and be thou here again 'ere the Leviathan can swim a league '."

Inspector Fox cast his eyes towards heaven and did as he was bid, returning with a roughed hare's foot.

" Thank you. Any luck with the hirelings?"

" Quite a bit," said Fox. " Surbonadier had been fooling round with the property man's girl, and she's Miss Vaughan's dresser, and her old man's Mr. Gardener's dresser."

" Oh, that."

" What do you mean, ' Oh that '?" asked Fox.

" I knew all that."

" How?"

" Props told me. Carry on with rest of 'em except Miss Vaughan, and Mr. Gardener. See them one by one. Find out where they all were during the black-out."

" Very good, sir," said Fox formally.

" And don't be cross with me, my Foxkin. You're doing well—excellent well, i'faith."

" Is that Shakespeare?"

" What if it is? Away you go."

" May I stay?" asked Nigel, as Fox went off.

" Do!" Alleyn took a small bottle and a rag from his bag and thoroughly cleaned the hare's foot. He then began to use it as a tiny broom, sweeping up what appeared to be dust from the floor, into a little phial out of the bag. " What have you found, Bailey?" he asked.

" Prints from Prop's rubber shoes, and Simpson's evening ones. Nobody else has stood right inside the prompt box."

"Well, I've got enough sand to be conclusive, if it tallies with what's in the blanks, and I think it will. Gosh, it's getting late!"

"Why the sand?" asked Nigel.

"Think. Think. Think."

"Oh, I see. If it's sand out of the cartridge case, it means Props did bring the dummies to Simpson and they must have been changed during the black-out."

"Stop laughing," said Alleyn to an imaginary audience. "The child's quite right. Now Bailey, will you get what you can in the way of prints from the revolver and the desk. Oh, lumme what a muddle it all is? Let's have a look at the cartridges in the revolver."

The revolver, held delicately by the extreme end of the barrel, was laid on a table. Bailey, using the insufflator, tested it for fingerprints and, referring to those he had already got, disclosed sufficiently clear evidence of Gardener, Surbonadier, and the dresser having handled it. They broke it open and Bailey turned his attention to the butt ends of the shells. The revolver was a Smith and Wesson and the cartridges ordinary .455. The ends yielded no prints, except Surbonardier's, neither did any other part of the cartridges nor the empty shell.

"Blast!" said Bailey.

"Couldn't expect anything else," said Alleyn philosophically. "Hullo—what's this?"

He picked up one cartridge and held it under a stage lamp. Nigel followed him hopefully. He took out his magnifying glass and looked through it at the shell. He did this with all the other cartridges.

"What is it?" asked Nigel.

Alleyn handed him the glass and he in turn examined the cartridges.

Alleyn waited.

"There's—there's a kind of whitish look," ventured Nigel, "on all of them. It's very faint on most, but here's one where it looks clearer. It looks almost like paint."

"Smell it."

"I can smell nothing but brass."

"Put your cigarette out. Blow your nose. Now smell."

"There *is* something else. It reminds me of something. What is it?"

"It looks like one person. It smells like another."

"What on earth do you mean?"

"It looks like cosmetic and it smells like Jacob Saint."

Chapter VIII

FELIX GARDENER

"What's the time?" said Alleyn, yawning.

"Nearly two o'clock and a dirty night."

"Oh, horror! I loathe late hours."

"Two's not late."

"Not for a journalist, perhaps. Hullo, here come the mummers."

Voices and footsteps sounded in the passage and presently a little procession appeared. Miss Dulcie Deamer, Mr. Howard Melville, Mr. J. Barclay Crammer, Inspector Fox. Miss Dulcie Deamer had her street make-up on— that is to say she had aimed a blow at her cheeks with the rouge puff, and had painted a pair of lips somewhere underneath her nose. She still contrived to be *jeune fille*. J. Barclay Crammer's face showed signs of No. 5 grease paint lingering round the eyebrows and a hint of rather pathetic grey stubble on the chin. He wore a plaid muffler, with one end tossed over his shoulder, and he looked profoundly disgusted. Mr. Melville was pale and anxious.

"Dulcie, how are you going home?" he asked querulously.

"Oh, my God, in a taxi!" she answered drearily.

"I live at Hampstead," Mr. Crammer intoned.

"We are very sorry about all this," said Alleyn, "and will, of course, make ourselves responsible for getting all of you home. The constable at the door will fix it up. Fox, just look after them, will you? Good night."

"*Good* night, everybody, *good* night," mimicked Mr.

Crammer bitterly. Miss Deamer glanced timidly and confidingly at Alleyn, who bowed formally. Mr. Melville said: "Oh—ah—good night." Alleyn glanced at him and seemed to get an idea.

"Half a minute, Mr. Melville," he said.

Mr. Melville instantly became green in the face.

"I'll only keep you a few moments," explained the inspector, "but we'll let the others go on, I think. Just wait for me in the wardrobe-room, will you?"

The others turned alarmed glances on Mr. Melville, who looked rather piteously after them and then returned to the wardrobe-room. They filed out towards the stage door.

"Fox," said Alleyn, "have they been searched?"

"The men have thoroughly. I—I kind of patted the lady. She's wearing hardly anything."

"Is there room for a glove there, do you think?"

"Oh—a glove. That's different."

"I know it is, and I've let two of 'em out without a complete search, benighted dolt and I am. Still, old Miss Max is really out of the picture, and there was nothing under those sequins except the Emerald. She doesn't wear stays."

"Nor does Dulcie," said Inspector Fox gloomily.

"Fox, we forget ourselves. If you're not sure, persuade her to go to the station and be searched there. If not, send 'em home in taxis and pay for them."

"Right-oh, sir."

"Where's Mr. Gardener?"

"Waiting for you in the deceased's dressing-room."

"Thank you. Are you coming, Bathgate, or do you yearn for your bed?"

"I'll come," said Nigel.

Felix Gardener stood in the middle of the doorway with his hands in his pockets. He started nervously when they came in and then gave a little laugh at himself.

"Is it an arrest?" he said jerkily.

"Not unless you are going to surprise me with a confession," said Alleyn cheerfully. "Let's sit down."

"A confession. My God, it's clear enough without that!

I shot him. No matter who planned this ghastly business, I shot him. I'll never get rid of that."

"If you are innocent, Mr. Gardener, you are entirely innocent. You are no more to blame than Mr. Simpson, who put the dummies, or it might have been the cartridges"— Nigel glanced at him in surprise—" in the drawer of the desk. You are as much an instrument as the revolver —as Surbonadier was himself, in loading it."

"I've been repeating that to myself over and over again, but it doesn't make much difference. Nigel, if you could have seen the way he looked at me—as if he knew—as if, in that tiniest fraction of time, he knew what had happened, and thought I'd done it. He looked so surprised. I didn't know myself at first. I got such a shock—you can't think—with the revolver going off. I just went on with the lines. It's Bill's revolver, you know. He said he never shot at a Hun with it. Good job he's dead and can't see all this. He fell just like he always did. Limp. Arthur played the part well. Didn't you think so? And you know I didn't like him. I said so, didn't I—this evening? Oh,. God !"

"Mr. Gardener, you can do no good by this," said Alleyn quietly. "Perhaps the truest of all our tiresome clichés is the one that says time cures all things. As a policeman, I should like to say 'time solves all things', but that unfortunately is not always the case. As a policeman I must ask you certain questions."

"You mean you want to find out if I did it on purpose?"

"I want to prove that you didn't. Where were you at the beginning of the first scene in the last act?"

"The first scene in the last act. You mean the scene when Arthur took the revolver and loaded it."

"That scene—yes. Where were you?"

"I was—where was I?—in my dressing-room."

"When did you come out?"

Gardener buried his face in his hands and then looked up helplessly.

"I don't know. I suppose soon after I was called. Let me think—I can't think collectedly at all. I was called, and I came out into the passage."

67

"When was this?"

"During the front scene, I think."

"Before or after the black-out, during which the first part of that scene is played?"

"I can't remember. I've really no recollection of anything that happened just before——"

"Some little thing may bring it back. Did you, for instance, walk out of the passage on to a pitch-black stage?"

"Somebody trod on my foot," said Gardener suddenly.

"Somebody trod on your foot—in the dark?"

"Yes. A man."

"Where was this?"

"In the wings—I don't quite know where—it was pitch dark."

"Any idea who it was?"

Gardener looked with quick apprehension at Nigel. "Shall I implicate anyone by this?"

"For Heaven's sake," said Nigel, "tell the truth."

Gardener was silent for a moment. "No," he said at last "If I had an idea, it was altogether too slight to be of use, and it would carry undue weight; you couldn't help yourself—you'd be influenced. I can see that. I've done enough harm for one night, haven't I?" He stared fiercely at Alleyn.

Alleyn smiled.

"I'm not terribly easily influenced," he said, "and I promise it won't carry one ounce overweight."

"No," said Gardener obstinately. "I'm not even sure myself. The more I think the less sure I get."

"Was it something to do with your sense of smell?"

"My God!" whispered Gardener.

"Thank you," said Alleyn.

Gardener and Nigel stared at him. Gardener began to laugh hysterically.

"Proper detective stuff. 'This man is clever.' Actor-proof part."

"Be quiet," said Alleyn. "I don't want any more histrionics. I'm sick of scenes, Mr. Gardener."

68

" Sorry."

" So I should hope. Now this revolver. I understand it belonged to you brother. How long have you had it, please?"

" Ever since he died."

" Had you any ammunition?"

" I gave Props the cartridges he turned into dummies."

" Any more at home?"

" No, couldn't find any more. Just the six that were in it. Oh, I supplied everything."

" What did you do after you ran into the man in the dark offstage?"

" Swore and rubbed my foot. It was still hurting when the lights went up."

" Did you go anywhere near the desk that was standing on the stage—almost in the wings?"

" I've no idea. I suppose I must have done so. You mean the desk that—the cartridges were in. It must have been close by."

" About that scene we all witnessed in Miss Vaughan's dressing-room. Why did Surbonadier make that very unpleasant to-do?"

" He was tight."

" Nothing else behind it?"

" He dislikes me. I told you that."

" So you did," agreed Alleyn. " But it seemed to me that he disliked you for more reason than that of professional jealousy."

" Yes. You must have seen how it was."

" Miss Vaughan?"

" At least, let us keep Stephanie out of this."

" She is in it. She must take her place in the jig-saw puzzle. I'm sorry. The nicer delicacies do not enter into murder cases. I take it you are engaged to Miss Vaughan and that Surbonadier was the unsuccessful suitor."

" We are not publicly engaged. *We're* not. I've no doubt killed my chances along with my only serious rival. The engagement was to be announced at our supper-party."

" Yes, I see. Mr. Gardener, have you a pair of gloves here in your dressing-room?"

Gardener turned very white.

"Yes," he said, "I have."

"Where?"

"I don't know. Probably in my overcoat pocket. I don't wear any in the piece."

Alleyn felt in the pockets of an overcoat that hung under the sheet. He found a pair of white wash-leather gloves which he examined very carefully. He smelt them, held them under the light, looked at each finger, and then threw them to Gardener.

"A perfectly innocent pair of gloves," he said. "Thank you, Mr. Gardener, I appreciate your frankness. Now, if you agree, I'm going to search you, as I have searched all the others."

Nigel watched this proceeding with the liveliest anxiety. He did not know what Alleyn expected to find, or, indeed, if he expected to find anything. He found nothing.

"That's all, Mr. Gardener," he said. "I'll keep you no longer."

"I'll wait if I may," said Gardener, "for Stephanie. She wanted me to see you first."

"Certainly. Wait on the stage, will you?"

"Shall I come?" asked Nigel diffidently.

"No thanks, old thing. If you don't mind I'd rather be alone."

He went out.

"Well?" asked Nigel anxiously.

"Well, Bathgate, we don't progress very fast. What's happened to your shorthand notes?"

"I—I couldn't report old Felix for you."

"I'm not quite a machine," said Alleyn gently. He raised his voice. "Got everything, Fox?"

"Everything O.K.," answered Inspector Fox from the next room. In a moment he appeared.

"He's been taking it down outside the door," said Alleyn. "I really can't trust my filthy memory."

"Oh, lord."

"Like to go home?" asked Alleyn.

"Not unless you want to get rid of me," said Nigel.

"Stay put then. Fox, you saw the dressers, Mr. and Miss Beadle?"

"Yes. The girl howled, and said she never done no harm to anybody, and that Mr. Surbonadier was always trying on his funny business, and that Props was her boy. Old Beadle said much the same. He'd warned the girl to look out for Mr. Surbonadier. They were both in the wardrobe-room during the black-out. Alone there together, they said. They met in the elbow of the passage, and went along together. She's a flighty bit of goods. I should say. Deceased was evidently"—Inspector Fox stopped and grimaced—"a nasty kind of chap. You might like to see the girl yourself, some time. The old father's a decent old bird and seems very fond of her."

"All right, I'll remember them. And now I'll have to see Miss Vaughan. I should have done so earlier and let her go home."

"She wanted the others to go first," said Fox. "I—took her clothes into the wardrobe-room and she said she'd change. She's not quite ready."

It was obvious from Inspector Fox's manner that he put Miss Vaughan in a superior catalogue to the rest of the cast. Alleyn looked at him and grinned.

"What's the joke?" inquired Fox suspiciously.

"No offence in the world. Have you carried on with routine work?"

"Mr. Melville helped Bailey re-set the scene in which the revolver was loaded. Haven't found the gloves."

"I'll just take a look at it while she's changing." They returned to the stage. Felix Gardener was walking up and down the passage to the outside exit, and paid little attention to them. Nigel went and spoke to Gardener, but he answered at random and looked at him as though they were strangers.

"It'll be all right, Felix," ventured Nigel lamely.

"What'll be all right?"

"Alleyn will find out who did it. Innocent people are never accused nowadays."

"Do you think I'm worrying about that?" asked Gar-

71

dener, and fell to walking up and down again. Nigel left him alone.

On the stage Alleyn looked critically at the reconstruction of the penultimate scene. The desk was in position. Miss Max's arm-chair was on the O.P. side, and the window-seat in position, near which Janet Emerald had had her last conversation with Arthur Surbonadier.

"We've had all the chair-seats out and so on," said Bailey, who was in shirt sleeves. The two constables, who had been helping him, stared solemnly at the furniture. Melville had gone.

"There's something missing," said Alleyn.

"Mr. Melville said not, sir," said Bailey.

"Yes, there is. A spot of colour. What is it?" He turned to Nigel. "There was a spot of colour somewhere in that scene. Something red."

"I know," said Nigel suddenly. "Miss Max's bag for her knitting. It hung on that chair arm."

"Good man," exclaimed Alleyn. "Let's find it." They hunted about. One of the constables disappeared in the direction of the property room.

"Damn the thing, where is it?" murmured Alleyn. "It hung on the chair throughout the scene, and at the end she stuffed her knitting into it and left it there." He hunted round offstage and muttered to himself.

"Does it matter much?" Nigel asked wearily.

"What?"

"Does it matter much?"

"No. I just want to make the stage look pretty."

Nigel was silent.

"Is this the affair, sir?" said the constable, reappearing. In his paw he held a large red bag. Alleyn strode over and took it.

"That's it."

He drew out a long and loud strip of knitting, and then thrust his hand deeper into the bag. A singularly blank look stole over his face, and others, who knew him, pricked up their ears.

"Has any gentleman in the audience missed an article of clothing?" asked Alleyn. He made a face at Nigel, and looked round, most provokingly. Then so suddenly that they all jumped, he whisked out his hand and held it high above his head.

In it was a pair of grey suède gloves. "Eureka!" said Chief Detective-Inspector Alleyn.

Chapter IX

STEPHANIE VAUGHAN'S SHOULDER

"Yes, but look here," Nigel began indignantly.

"Old Miss Max—I mean to say, that's a bit too thick. She's a nice old thing."

Alleyn gave one of his rare laughs. "All right, all right," he said. "Don't bite my head off. I didn't plant the things."

"Well, somebody else did, then,"

"Quite possible. During the black-out. Oh, it's a very nasty bit of goods, this is. And so clever, so filthily clever. Everything nice and simple. No fancy touches. I tell you one thing, all of you, for what it's worth. I've been telling it to myself ever since this started. We're up against good acting."

"Yes," said Nigel thoughtfully, "the very best."

"As you say. It's a West End production, bad luck to it."

"Anything on the thumb of the right-hand glove?" asked Fox abruptly.

Alleyn picked it up by one finger.

"Oh, Mr. Fox, aren't you wonderful?" he said. "Such a lovely quality, moddom, or, rather, sir. Yes, definitely, 'sir.' Have a sniff." He held them out.

"I've got it," said Fox. "They smell of cigars, and scent, and—damn it —where did I smell that scent?"

"On Mr. Jacob Saint."

"By gum, you're right, sir."

"It's a very good scent. Something rather special. But how careless of Mr. Saint to lose his gloves, how rather surprisingly careless." He handed the glove over to his colleague.

"When were they lost? He was wearing none when he came round," Fox declared. "I know that because he shoved me aside at the door, and his ring dug into my hand."

"His altogether too big signet ring," murmured Alleyn. "It does dig in. Look!"

He held up the little finger of the left-hand glove. The base showed a distinct bulge.

"He was behind the scenes earlier in the evening, you know. Before the curtain went up. Then he was in front."

"Could he have come round again, later?" asked Nigel.

"We must find out. By George, Fox, what happened to the old gentleman?"

"Who's he?"

"The stage door-keeper."

"I never saw one. He must have gone home during the first few moments."

"He was there when we came round. Not very good. He'll have to be traced. Oh well, let's have Miss Vaughan. I think I'll see her alone, if you please, Fox. There's nothing much else to be done here that I can think of. Have you looked closely at the thumb?"

"Yes," said Fox carefully. "There's a bit of whitish stain on it."

"There is, indeed. We may want an analysis of that to compare with the cartridges."

"What do you make it out to be?"

"Oh, cosmetic, Fox, cosmetic. While I'm talking to Miss Vaughan, see if you two can match it in any of the dressing-rooms. Take samples of any make-up that looks like it and note where from, and all that. And now would you take my compliments to Miss Vaughan and ask her if she would be kind enough to come out here?"

Fox and Bailey went off. Presently the constable who had been stationed outside the wardrobe-room came back and with a glance at Alleyn disappeared in the direction of the stage door. Alleyn followed him, said something that Nigel did not catch and returned.

"Any objection to noting this down for me?" asked Alleyn.

"No," said Nigel. "If I had any, they are overruled by curiosity. I'll go back to my cache-cache."

"Thank you. Here she comes."

Nigel slipped through the doorway in the set. He discovered that, by moving his seat, he could leave the door half open and get a fuller view of the stage without being visible. In this way he was able to see Stephanie Vaughan when she came on to the scene. She had changed her dress and was wearing a dark fur wrap. The stage make-up was gone, and she looked pale and rather tired. There was no hint of histrionics in her manner now. She was grave and dignified, and a little remote. "Why, it's not the same woman," thought Nigel.

"You sent for me," she said quietly.

"I'm sorry if my message sounded peremptory," answered Alleyn.

"Why not? You're in charge."

"Will you sit down?"

She sank into an arm-chair, and there was a little silence.

"What do you want to ask me?" she said at last.

"Several questions. The first—where were you during the black-out at the beginning of the last act?"

"In my dressing-room, changing. Then I went in to see Felix."

"Was anyone with you? In your own room, I mean?"

"My dresser."

"All the time?"

"I've no idea. From my dressing-room I couldn't see when the stage lights went on."

"I should have thought you could hear the dialogue."

"Possibly, I didn't listen."

"Was Mr. Gardener still in his room when you left it?"

"No. He went out first. He came on before I did."

"When did you go out on to the stage?"

"When the scene was over."

"Yes. Thank you. What happened after Bathgate and I left your dressing-room?"

The question must have taken her by surprise. Nigel heard her draw in her breath. When she spoke, however, her voice was quite even.

"After you left," she said, "there was a scene."

"There was the making of one while we were there. What happened?"

She leant back wearily, her wrap slipped down. She winced, as if something had hurt her, and sat forward again, pulling the fur collar over her shoulders.

"You are hurt?" said Alleyn. "Your shoulder. You put your hand up to it."

"Arthur hit me."

"What!"

"Oh, yes."

"Let me see it."

She let her wrap fall, and pulled aside her dress, hunching up her shoulder. Nigel could see the bruise. Alleyn bent over her without touching her.

"What did Gardener do?"

"He wasn't there. I'm beginning half-way, I suppose. The moment you had gone I made Felix leave me. He didn't want to, of course, but I had to deal with Arthur alone, and I insisted. He didn't like going, but he went."

"And then?"

"And then there was a scene—a scene in a whisper. We had had them before. I was used to it. He was quite beside himself with jealousy, and threatened me with all sorts of things. Then he became maudlin and shed tears. I'd never seen him like that before."

"With what did he threaten you?"

"He told me," said Miss Vaughan gently, "that he would drag my name in the mud. He said he would stop Felix marrying me. Really, if Felix had been shot, I should not have wondered. Arthur looked murderous. I think he did it himself."

"Do you? Had he that sort of rogue's courage?"

"I think so. He hoped Felix would be accused."

76

"Where was he," asked Alleyn, "when he struck you?"

"How do you mean? I was sitting where you left me —on the small chair in my room. He was standing, I think, about as far off as you are now."

"With his left hand, then?"

"No. I don't know. I can't remember, I'm afraid. Perhaps if you were to do it—but gently, please—I might remember."

Alleyn moved his right arm and Nigel saw his hand against the left side of her throat.

"It would be there, on your face," he said. "I think it must have been with his left hand, and even then it would be a strange sort of blow."

"He was drunk."

"So everyone keeps telling me. Could he not have been behind you? Like this."

Alleyn stood behind her and laid his right hand on her right shoulder. Nigel was suddenly and vividly reminded of the scene in the dressing-room, when Gardener had stood, touching her in the same way, and laughing at Alleyn's remark about Edgar Wallace.

"My hand falls exactly over the bruise," said Alleyn. "Am I hurting you?"

"No."

"Let me draw up your wrap. You are cold."

"Thank you."

"Do you think that could have been the way of it?"

"Perhaps. He was lurching about the room. I really don't remember."

"You must have been terrified."

"No. He was not a terrifying man, but I was glad Felix had gone. I managed to get rid of Arthur and then I went to Felix's room."

"Next door?"

"Yes. I said nothing about the blow on my shoulder. Beadle was there but left as soon as I went in. Then I told Felix it had all petered out."

"What did he say"

"He said that Arthur was a drunken pig, but that in a way he was sorry for him. He said I must let him speak

77

to Master Surbonadier and tell him to behave himself, and that he wouldn't have me worried like that."

"Quite temperate about it?"

"Yes. He knew that sort of thing didn't really count and we both had a horror of more scenes. We only spoke a few words, and then Felix went out on to the stage. The lights were still out, I remember. Have you got a cigarette, Mr. Alleyn? I should like one."

"I'm very sorry. I didn't think."

She took one from his case and he lit it for her. She touched her fingers against the back of his hand, and they seemed to look full in each other's face. Then she leant back again in her chair. They smoked in silence for a little time—Alleyn very composedly, Miss Vaughan not so composedly.

"Please tell me this," she said at last, very earnestly, "do you suspect anyone?"

"You cannot expect me to answer that," said Alleyn.

"Why not?"

"Everyone is under suspicion. Everyone is lying and acting."

"Even me? Have I lied or played a part?"

"I don't know," said Alleyn sombrely. "How should I?"

"How you dislike me, Inspector Alleyn!"

"You think so?" said Alleyn swiftly, and then, after a pause: "Do you ever do jig-saw puzzles?"

"Sometimes."

"And do you ever conceive an ardent distaste for a bit that won't fit in?"

"Yes."

"That is the only kind of personal prejudice a policeman can allow himself. I have that feeling for the pieces that don't fit. For the ones that do, I develop a queer sort of affection."

"And you can't fit me into your puzzle?"

"On the contrary, I think I have you—just where you belong."

"My cigarette is finished. Have you anything more to ask me? No, I don't want another."

78

"Only one more point. May I have your hand?"

She held out both her hands. Nigel was astonished to see him take them very lightly in his, and raise them to his face. He turned them over in his palms, and stood with his eyes closed, his lips almost touching them. She made no attempt to withdraw them, but she was less pale, and Nigel thought her hands trembled very slightly. Then he let them drop.

"Chanel No. 5," he said. "Thank you very much, Miss Vaughan."

She hid her hands swiftly in the fur sleeves of her coat. "I thought you were going to kiss them," she said lightly.

"I trust I know my place," said Alleyn, "Good night. Mr. Gardener is waiting for you."

"Good night. Do you want my address?"

"Please."

"Flat 10, The Nun's House, Shepherd's Market. Will you write it down?"

"There is no need. Good night."

She looked at him an instant and then went down the passage to the stage door. Nigel heard her calling:

"There you are, Felix"—and in a moment her footsteps had died away.

"Have you got that address down, Bathgate?" asked Alleyn anxiously.

"You old devil," said Nigel.

"Why?"

"Well. I don't know. I thought you didn't like her before, in the dressing-room."

"So did she."

"Now I'm not so sure."

"Nor is she."

"Are you being a cad, Mr. Alleyn?"

"Yes, Mr. Bathgate."

"What were you driving at about that bruise?"

"Didn't you guess? Can't you see?"

"No, I can't. Unless you wanted an excuse to dally with the lady"

"Have it that way, if you like," said Alleyn.

" I think you're very silly," said Nigel, grandly, " and I'm going home."

" So am I. Thank you for giving me such a lovely evening."

" Not a bit. So glad you were able to come. I must do a job of work before I go to bed."

" What's this—what's this?"

" Story for my paper. It's a scoop."

" You'll bring whatever gup you write to me in the morning, young fella."

" Oh, I say, Alleyn!" Nigel protested.

" Yes, indeed. I'd forgotten your horrible evening shocker. The officer outside has turned away a collection of your boy friends already."

" Well, let me do a bit. It's a scoop—really it is."

" Bring it to my study to-morrow morning, sir."

" Oh, all right."

Alleyn assembled his men and they filed out of the stage door. The lights were turned off.

" A final black-out," said Alleyn's voice in the dark.

The stage of the Unicorn was completely silent and quite given over to the memory of dead plays. Nigel was oppressed by the sense of uneasy expectation that visits all interlopers in deserted buildings. Now, he thought, was the time for the ghosts of old mummers to step out from behind the waiting doorways and mouth their way silently through forgotten scenes. Somewhere above their heads a rope creaked, and a little draught of air soughed among the hanging canvas.

" Let's go," said Nigel.

Alleyn switched on an electric torch and they found their way down the passage to the stage door. Nigel stepped out into the cool air. The others were talking to a night-watchman, and to two young men, whom Nigel recognised as journalists.

" Just a moment," said Alleyn's voice in the passage. " Look here!"

The others turned back. The light from the torch had penetrated a kind of dark cubby-hole on the left of the doorway. It shone on old Blair's closed eyes.

"Good God!" exclaimed Nigel. "Is he dead?"

"No—only asleep," said Alleyn. "What's his name?"

"Blair," said the night-watchman.

"Wake up, Blair," said Alleyn. "It's long past the final curtain, and they've all gone home to bed."

Chapter X

THE DAY AFTER

By nine o'clock on the following morning Nigel had got his story ready to go to press. He warned his sub-editors of his activities and they agreed, with a certain display of irritated enthusiasm, to hold back the front page while he submitted his copy to Alleyn. The morning papers were blazing with effective headlines, supported by exceedingly meagre information. Nigel sought out his friend at Scotland Yard and found him more amenable to persuasion than he had anticipated. The article laid great emphasis on the view that Gardener's part in the tragedy, painful though it had been for himself, did not point in any way to his complicity in the murder. Alleyn did not dispute this, or censor a word of it. Nigel had made little of the personal relationships of Surbonadier, Gardener and Miss Vaughan, beyond using the romantic appeal of the engagement between the last two. He made a lot of his first-hand impression of the tragedy, and of the subsequent scenes behind the curtain.

"Less culpable than I anticipated," said Chief Detective-Inspector Alleyn. "With the few deletions I've pencilled it can go through. Are you returning to your office?"

"Not if you'll have me here," said Nigel promptly. "I've got a boy to take back the copy."

"Aren't you a one? All right—come back. I've come to the stage when I can do with a Boswell."

"Throwing bouquets at yourself, I see," said Nigel. "I'll be back in a jiffy."

Having sent the boy off to Fleet Street, he returned to find Alleyn at the telephone.

"Very well," he said into the instrument as he glanced round at Nigel, "I'll see you in twenty minutes"—and hung up the receiver.

"A very unpleasant gentleman," he grunted.

"How—unpleasant?"

"An informer, or hopes to be."

"Who is it?"

"Mr. Saint's footman. Wait and see."

"I will," said Nigel enthusiastically. "How are you getting on, inspector?"

"Oh, it's a devil of a job," Alleyn complained.

"I've been trying to get it straight in my mind," ventured Nigel, "as far as I know it. I made a sort of amateur dossier."

"I don't suppose you know what a dossier is," said Alleyn. "However, let's see your effort."

Nigel produced several sheets of typewritten paper.

"Here are the notes I took for you."

"Thank you so much, Bathgate. Now do show me your summary. It may be very useful. I'm bad at summarising."

Nigel glanced suspiciously at him, but Alleyn seemed to be quite serious. He lit his pipe and applied himself to the sheet of foolscap, at the top of which Nigel had typed in capital letters:

MURDER AT THE UNICORN

"*Circumstances.* Surbonadier was shot by Gardener with the revolver used in the piece. According to the evidence of the stage manager and the property man, dummy cartridges, of which one was faulty, were placed in the drawer of the desk, immediately before the scene in which Surbonadier loaded the gun. Traces of sand, found in the prompt box, seem to support this theory."

"There was also sand in the top drawer," said Alleyn, glancing up.

"Was there? That's pretty conclusive, then."

Alleyn read on:

"Props says the faulty cartridge only went wrong that
night, when he dropped it. Unless he is lying, and he
and the stage manager are in collusion, that means the
dummies were in the top drawer just before the scene
opened. Therefore the murderer substituted the lethal
cartridges either immediately prior to, or during, the
black-out, which lasted four minutes. He used gloves,
took the dummies from the top drawer, substituted the
real ones, put the dummies in the lower drawer, and got
rid of the gloves. A pair of men's grey suède gloves
was found in the bag that hung on an arm-chair on the
stage. Surbonadier took the cartridges from the top
drawer and loaded the revolver. During the scene that
followed Gardener took the gun from him and fired
point-blank in the usual way. The cartridges afterwards
found in the gun were all live ones.

"*Opportunity.* Everyone behind the scenes had the
chance of changing the cartridges. The people on the stage,
perhaps, had the greatest opportunity. These were Miss
Max, Miss Emerald, Surbonadier himself, and the stage
manager. On the other hand, anyone may have come
out on to the darkened stage and done it. Miss Vaughan,
Barclay Crammer, Howard Melville, Miss Deamer, the
dressers and the staff, all come under the heading.

"*Motive.* The characters involved may now be taken
in turn.

"*Miss Emerald.* She was on the stage. She had an
altercation with Surbonadier. She was seen by the S.M.
and Miss Max to cross to the desk and lean over it. Told
lies. Motive.—Unknown, but she had quarrelled with S.
N.B.—She seems to be on *very* friendly terms with Jacob
Saint, uncle of S.

"*Miss Max.* On the stage. Handled bag where gloves
were found. Did not go near desk while lights were up.
Motive.—None known.

"*Stage Manager.* On the stage. Handled dummy cartridges. Would be able to go to desk unnoticed or during
black-out. Peculiar witness. Motive—None known.

"*Property Master*. Handed dummies to S.M. Easy access to desk after black-out. Behaved suspiciously after murder. Dropped candelabrum from above. Hid in gallery. Concealed locality of dummies in second drawer. Motive. —Engaged to Trixie Beadle. Surbonadier had interfered with her. Shellshock case.

"*Stephanie Vaughan*. In dressing-room. Says Trixie Beadle, her dresser, was there with her, but can't remember how long. Says she went to Gardener's room and remained there until after the black-out. Motive.—Had been threatened by Surbonadier, who was madly in love with her. Possibly afraid of something he might reveal to Gardener. Engaged to Gardener.

"*Felix Gardener*. Fired the revolver. His own weapon Admits he came on to stage during black-out. Says someone trod on his foot. Supplied cartridges that Props converted into dummies. Motive.—Possibly Surbonadier's threats to Miss Vaughan.

"*J. B. Crammer*.
"*Dulcie Deamer*. ⎫ See Fox's report."
"*Howard Melville*. ⎭

Alleyn looked up.

"Didn't you hear? Melville and Crammer were together in Crammer's room during the black-out. Before that Melville had been on the stage. Miss Deamer was next door and heard their voices. I'll write it in for you."

He went on with the summary.

"See Fox's report. Motive.—None, except professional jealousy in Barclay Crammer's case.

"*Trixie Beadle*. Was helping Miss Vaughan, but told Fox she was with her father in wardrobe-room during black-out. May have gone there from dressing-room. Motive.—Had possibly been seduced by deceased, and was afraid of him telling Props. Engaged to Props.

"*Beadle*. Father of above. Told Fox he was in wardrobe-room with his daughter. Met daughter in passage first. Motive.—Surbonadier meddling with the girl.

"*Old Blair*. Stage door-keeper. Most unlikely.

" *Jacob Saint.* Owns the show. Was behind earlier in the evening. Deceased's uncle. Had a row with him. Hypothetical owner of the gloves found in bag. Gardener seemed to remember noticing a scent on the person who trod on his foot. Saint uses a very noticeable scent. Motive. —Unknown, except for the row about casting.

" *Stage Staff.* All in the property-room.

" *Notes.* Points of interest. Janet Emerald exclaimed : ' It wasn't you. They can't say it was you,' when Saint appeared. She lied about herself. Props behaved very strangely and suspiciously. Was Miss Vaughan telling the truth? Had Saint come back on to the stage? At first-night party Barclay Crammer seemed to dislike Surbonadier intensely. I noticed coolness between Saint and Surbonadier at studio party."

Here Nigel's document ended abruptly. Alleyn laid it down on his desk.

" It's all quite correct," he approved. " It's even rather suggestive. If you were a policeman, what would you do. next?"

" I haven't any idea."

" Really? Well, I'll tell you what we have done. We've been delving in the murky past of Mr. Jacob Saint."

" Jimini !"

" Yes. Rather a chequered career. You can help me."

" I say—can I really?"

" How long have you been a Pressman?"

" Ever since I came down from Cambridge."

" Almost the G.O.M. of Fleet Street. It's a matter of a year, isn't it?"

" And three months."

" Then you don't remember the illicit drug scandal of some six years ago, and an article in the *Morning Express* that resulted in a libel action in which Jacob Saint featured as plaintiff, and triumphed to the tune of five thousand pounds?"

Nigel whistled shrilly and then became thoughtful. " I do remember vaguely," he said.

" The case was spectacular. The article hinted pretty

broadly that Saint's fortune had been amassed through the rather wholesale supply of proscribed drugs. Ladies and gentlemen with unattractive portmanteaux under their yellow eyeballs were, said the writer, constantly being obliged with opium and cocaine by some agency controlled by a 'well-known theatre magnate whose recent successes in a playhouse not a thousand yards from Piccadilly . . .' and so on. As I have said, Saint took it to court, won hands down, and emerged a little tarnished but triumphant. One very curious fact came out. The identity of the author was unknown. A leading reporter on the *Morning Express* was away on holiday. The article arrived at the office purporting to have come from him. A typewritten note was signed with a clever forgery of his name. He denied any knowledge of the business and made his case good. For once in its cocksure career, the *Morning Express* had been had. The address on the notepaper was 'Mossburn,' a village near Cambridge, and the postmark, noticed by the secretary, bore this out. A half-hearted attempt was made to trace the authorship, but in any case the 'Mex,' as I believe your journalists call it, was responsible. Mr. Saint was dreadfully annoyed, and, oh, so virtuous."

"What's all this leading to?"

"The postmark was of a village near Cambridge."

"Are you thinking of Felix?" said Nigel hotly.

"Of Gardener? Where was he this time six years ago?" Nigel paused. He eyed Alleyn uncomfortably. "Well, since you must know," he said at last, "he had just gone up to Cambridge. He was two years ahead of me."

"I see."

"Look here—what are you thinking?"

"I'm only wondering. That article reads like undergraduate stuff. There's an unmistakable flavour."

"Suppose there is? What are you driving at?"

"Literally only this. Gardener may possibly be able to throw some light on the matter."

"Oh, if that's all——" Nigel looked relieved. "I thought you meant he might have written it."

86

Alleyn looked curiously at him.

"That particular year," he said, "Surbonadier was sent down from Cambridge."

"*Surbonadier?*" said Nigel slowly.

"Yes," said Alleyn. "Now do you see?"

"You mean—you mean Surbonadier may have written the article and, therefore, knew too much about his uncle."

"That is possible."

"Yes."

"The catch in it is that all this happened six years ago."

"He may."

The telephone rang. Alleyn took off the receiver. "Yes. Who? Oh, send him up, will you?" He turned to Nigel. "This may help," he said.

"Who is it?"

"Mr. Jacob Saint's footman."

"The informer."

"Yes. I hate this sort of thing. He's going to make me feel ashamed."

"Really? You don't want me to go?"

"Stay where you are. Have a cigarette, and look as if you belonged. Have you seen Gardener this morning?"

"No, I'm going to ring him up. I'm afraid he's not going to forget this business in a hurry."

"I don't suppose so. Would you, in his place?"

"Never. But I think I'd worry a bit more about whether the police thought me guilty. It's the shock of having fired the revolver that seems to have got him down."

"Isn't that what you'd expect in an innocent man?"

"I'm glad to hear you call him that," said Nigel warmly.

"I talk a great deal too much," declared Alleyn. "Come in!"

The door opened to admit a tall, thin, and rather objectionably good-looking man. His face was a little too pale, his eyes were a little too large, and his mouth a little too soft. He closed the door tenderly, and stood quietly inside it.

"Good morning," said Alleyn.

"Good morning, sir."

"You wanted to see me in reference to the murder of Mr. Arthur Surbonadier."

"I thought you might wish to see me, sir."

"Why?"

The footman glanced at Nigel. Alleyn paid no attention to this indication of caution.

"Well?" he said.

"If I might inquire, sir, whether a little inside information about the late Mr. Surbonadier's relationships with my employer——"

"Oh," Alleyn cut him short, "you want to make a statement."

"Oh, no, sir. I only wanted to inquire. I don't want to mix myself up in anything unpleasant, sir. On the other hand, there was an incident that might be worth the police's while."

"If you are withholding any evidence that may be of value to the police, you will get into quite serious trouble. If you are expecting a bribe, however——"

"Oh, please, sir."

"You won't get one. Should your information be relevant you'll be called as a witness, and you'll be paid for that."

"Well, sir," said the man, with an angry smirk, "I must say you're very outspoken."

"I should advise you to follow my example."

The footman thought for a moment, and shot a rather apprehensive glance at the inspector.

"It's merely an incident," he said at last.

"Let's have it," said Alleyn. "Will you take it down for me, Bathgate?"

Nigel moved up to the desk.

"I understand you are a footman in the employ of Mr. Jacob Saint."

"Yes, sir. Or rather I was."

"Name?"

"Joseph Mincing. Age twenty-three. Address 299A,

88

Hanover Square," volunteered Mr. Mincing, with a little burst of frankness.

"Tell me, in your own words, what this incident was."

"It took place a month ago before this play come on. The twenty-fifth of May to be exact. I took special notice. It was in the afternoon. Mr. Surbonadier came to see Mr. Saint. I showed him into the library and waited outside in the 'all. Angry words passed, of which I heard many." Mr. Mincing paused and looked self-conscious.

"Yes?" said Alleyn.

"My attention was first aroused by hearing Mr. Surbonadier say very loud that he knew why Mr. Saint had paid Mr. Mortlake two thousand pounds. This seemed to make Mr. Saint very wild, sir. He didn't speak so loud at first, but his tones are penetrating at the best of times. Mr. Surbonadier says : 'I'll do it,' very defiant, and over and over again. I rather gathered, sir, that he was using pressure to force Mr. Saint to give him another part in the play. At first Mr. Saint took on something dreadful and ordered Mr. Surbonadier out, but presently they settled down a bit and spoke quieter and more reasonable."

"You still heard them, however?"

"Not everything. Mr. Saint seemed to promise Mr. Surbonadier a leading part in the next production, saying he couldn't alter this one. They argued a bit, and then it was settled. I heard Mr. Saint say he'd left his money to Mr. Surbonadier sir. 'Not all of it,' he says. 'Janet gets some, and if you go first she gets the lot.' They looked at the will, sir."

"How do you know?"

"Mr. Saint came out with Mr. Surbonadier later on, and I saw it on the desk."

"And read it?"

"Just glanced, as you might say, sir. I was familiar with it, in a manner of speaking. The butler and me had witnessed it the week before. It was quite short and on those lines—two thousand pounds a years to Miss Emerald, and the rest to Mr. Surbonadier, and a few legacies. The fortune was to go to Miss Emerald if Mr. Surbonadier was no more."

" Anything else?"

" They seemed to get quieter after that. Mr. Surbonadier said something about sending back a letter when the next piece was cast. Soon after that he left."

" Were you with Mr. Saint six years ago?"

" Yes, sir. As knife boy."

" Used Mr. Mortlake to call on him then?"

The man looked surprised. " Yes, sir."

" But not recently?"

" Very occasionally."

" Why did you get the sack?"

" I—I beg pardon, sir?"

" I think you heard what I said."

" Through no fault of my own," said Mincing sullenly.

" I see. Then you bear him a grudge?"

" No wonder if I do."

" Who is Mr. Jacob Saint's doctor?"

" His doctor, sir?"

" Yes."

"Er—it's Sir Everard Sim, sir."

" Has he been called in lately?"

" He comes in, quite regular."

" I see. No other information or incidents? Then you may go. Wait outside for half an hour. There will be a statement for you to sign."

" Thank you, sir."

The man opened the door quietly. He hesitated a moment and then said softly:

" Mr. Saint—he fair hated Mr. Surbonadier."

He went out, closing the door very gently after him.

Chapter XI

NIGEL TURNS SLEUTH

"That's a pretty little pet," said Alleyn. "There's a typewriter over there. Do you mind putting those squiggles into language?"

"Of course I will. Who's Mortlake?"

"He's a most elusive gentleman whom we have been brooding over for some years. At the time of the libel case his name wasn't even mentioned, but it fairly hummed between the lines. He's a Yank, and his pet names are 'Snow' and 'Dopey.'"

"Golly! It looks rum for Saint, doesn't it?"

"Yes, doesn't it? Get on with your typing."

"If he did it," announced Nigel, above the rattle of the machine, "he must have come round a second time, behind the scenes."

"And old Blair swears he didn't. I spoke to him last night while you were hunting up the taxi."

"May have been asleep."

"Says he wasn't. Says he retired to his cubby-hole, after we had gone through, and waited there. The bluebottle at the door thought he was with the others on the stage."

"Funny. Blair didn't speak to the bluebottle."

"I thought so too. He said he believed in keeping himself to himself, and such a thing had never happened before at the Unicorn."

"Why did you ask about Saint's doctor?"

"I wanted to know if the dear old gentleman was enjoying bonny health."

"Oh, rats!"

"I did. He looks like a heart subject. Such rosy cheeks."

Nigel returned, in exasperation, to his typing.

"There," he said presently. "That's done."

Alleyn touched a bell and brought forth a constable. "Is Mincing out there? The man I saw just now?"

"He is, sir."

"Read this through to him and get him to sign it. Then let him go. He's a horrid man."

"Very good, sir." The constable grinned and withdrew.

"Now, Bathgate," began Alleyn. "If you really want to be a help, there's something you can do for me. You can find out who the journalist was whose name was taken in vain over that article. Seek him out and do a bit of ferreting. Discover, if you can, any connection between him and the characters in our cast. See if he knew Surbonadier or Gardener—wait a moment; don't be so touchy—and if either of them is likely to have introduced him to the other. Got that?"

"Yes. I suppose I'll find his name in the files."

"The report of the case will give it. Hullo! Come in!" Detective-Sergeant Bailey put his head round the door.

"Busy, inspector?" he inquired.

"Not if it's the Unicorn case."

"It is," announced Bailey. He came in and, at Alleyn's invitation, sat down. Nigel kept quiet and hoped to hear something.

"It's the report on the cartridges," began Bailey. "The white stain was stuff used by Miss Vaughan. It's in a bottle labelled 'Stage-White'! It has been upset, but there was plenty left, and quite enough for the analyst on the glove. All the ladies used some sort of stuff, but hers was different. Specially made up for her. I've seen the chemist."

"And the same on the thumb of the glove?"

"Yes. It beats me, sir. What would she want to dong him off for? I reckoned it was the other lady."

"Your exquisite reason, Bailey?"

"Well, look how she carried on," said Bailey disgustedly. "Making a break for her dressing-room and lying away like a good 'un. Now I've seen the statements it looks still more like it."

"And she's one step nearer Mr. Saint's fortune by

this—she was his heir after the deceased. And Mr. Saint consults a heart specialist regularly and, no doubt, does not obey his orders. That makes your eyes bulge, doesn't it?"

"I must say it does, sir. Now look at it this way. Suppose my lady Emerald takes Mr. Saint's glove when he's round behind. She's sure to meet him, seeing how things are between them. She plants the gloves and the cartridges somewhere—likely enough in one of the unused drawers of the desk. She's on the stage. She's by the desk. She waits for the lights to be blacked out and then puts on the glove, changes over the cartridges, and drops the gloves in Miss Max's bag. It would look too obvious to leave them near the desk. She knows all this stuff about bad blood between Saint and his nephew will come out. Saint gets rigged out with the hug-me-tight necktie, and she romps home with the dibs."

"Could anything be better put? And I suppose she dips the thumb of the glove into Miss Vaughan's wet-white just to make if more difficult."

"That's the catch in it," admitted Bailey gloomily.

"Look here," said Nigel loudly. "Listen!"

"Ssh!" whispered Alleyn excitedly.

"Don't be silly, now. Listen to me. Miss Vaughan showed you how Surbonadier struck her on the shoulder. Suppose he got the stuff on his hand and—oh no. Sorry."

"As we were, Bailey," said Alleyn.

"We all of us make mistakes, sir," said Detective Bailey kindly.

Nigel looked foolish.

"Well, anyway," he said, "I bet Surbonadier upset the stuff."

"More than likely," agreed Alleyn.

At this juncture Inspector Fox walked in.

"Here's the Props fancier," said Alleyn.

"Good morning, Mr. Bathgate. Yes, that's me. I don't see how you can get past the funny business with the chandelier. And he *knew* the dummies were in the second drawer. There's motive, behaviour and everything else."

"And the gloves?" Alleyn asked.

"Left on the stage by Mr. Saint, and used by Props for the job."

"And the stage-white of Miss Vaughan, on the glove of Mr. Saint, used by Props for the job?"

"Oh, it was hers, was it?" grumbled Inspector Fox. "Well, Saint must have gone into her room."

"It's ingenious, Fox," said Alleyn, "but I don't think it's quite right. I take it, this stage-white dries like a particularly clinging powder. Now if Saint had got it on his glove, earlier in the evening, it would be dry when the glove was used for the cartridges, and if any came off, it would be powdery and not likely to stick to the brass. Through the lens those marks looked as if the stuff had been smeared on, wet."

"The same thing applies to Felix," ventured Nigel. "According to Miss Vaughan, he left her room soon after we did, and after that they only met in his room."

Alleyn swung round slowly.

"That's quite true," he said; "leaving her room vacant, during the black-out."

"I get you," said Fox heavily.

"I don't," confessed Nigel.

"Don't you? Well I'm jolly well going to be inscrutable. The next thing to do is to see Mr. Jacob Saint again. He *said* he might call in. Do you know, I believe I'll ask the old darling. Run and do your job, Bathgate."

"Oh, I say," Nigel protested. "Can't I wait and hear Uncle Jacob?"

"Away you go!"

Nigel attempted persuasion and was cheerfully invited to get out before he was thrown out. He departed conscious of smiles on the faces of Inspector Fox and Detective-Sergeant Bailey. A hunt through the file in his own office rewarded him with a complete account of the Jacob Saint libel action, and the discovery of the reporter's name. He was one Edward Wakeford, whom Nigel knew slightly and who was now literary editor on the staff of a weekly paper. Nigel rang him up and arranged a meeting in the bar of a Fleet Street tavern much patronised by

Pressmen. They forgathered at eleven o'clock, and over enormous tankards of lager the subject of the trial was broached.

"You doing this Unicorn murder?" asked Wakeford.

"Yes, I am. I know Alleyn, of the Yard, and was with him at the show. It was a marvellous chance, but, of course, I have to play fair. He vets everything."

"By George, he's a marvel, that man," said Wakeford; "I could tell you of a case"—and did.

"It was Alleyn who asked me to look you up," Nigel told him. "He wants to know if you've any idea who wrote the article in the 'Mex' in the Saint libel action. The story that was supposed to be yours."

Wakeford reply was startling. "I've always thought it was Arthur Surbonadier," he said.

"Gosh, Wakeford—this—this is simply terrific, honestly it is! Why did you think so?"

"Oh, I've nothing much to go on, but I knew the blighter and I'd written to him, so he could have forged my signature. He was Saint's nephew and likely enough to have inside information."

"But why would he do it? Old Saint paid for his education, and gave him everything he had."

"They never got on though. And Surbonadier was always in debt. By the way, he wasn't 'Surbonadier' in those days. He was Arthur Simes. Saint's name is Simes, you know. Arthur crashed heavily soon after that, and was sent down. It was a very unsavoury business. Then Uncle Jacob gave him a chance on the boards and he hurriedly changed to 'Surbonadier.'"

"And he wasn't paid for the article?"

"No, of course not."

"Then I don't see why——"

"Nor can I, except that he was an extraordinary vindictive sort of chap, and was drinking heavily, even then."

"Didn't Saint suspect him?"

"Saint always swore that forgery was a ramp and that the story was written by me. Legally it didn't arise.

95

The 'Mex' was responsible, whoever wrote the stuff, and, thank the Lord, they believed me. It wasn't quite my style, but it wasn't a bad imitation."

"Have you ever met Felix Gardener?"

"No. Why?"

"He's a friend of mine. It's a ghastly situation for him."

"Awful. But the police don't suspect him, surely?"

"No, I'm sure they don't. But, you see, he did actually shoot Surbonadier. It's an unpleasant thought for him."

"Oh, terrible, I quite agree. Well, that's all I can do to help you. What do I get? It's not my line or I'd pinch your story."

Nigel gave him a friendly but rather absentminded punch.

"Felix must have been a freshman when it happened. I wonder if he could let any light in on it himself. He may have known Surbonadier."

"Try him. I must push off."

"I'm terribly obliged to you, Wakeford."

"Not a bit. Bung-oh," said Wakeford genially, and went his ways.

Nigel was in two minds whether to rush of to Alleyn with his booty, or to seek out Gardener with what, he could not help feeling, was a piece of heartening news. In the end he plumped for Gardener and, in the fury of his zest, took a taxi to the studio-flat in Sloane Street.

Gardener was in. Nigel found him looking wretchedly lost and miserable. He had apparently been staring out of his window, and turned from there with a terribly startled face as Nigel walked in.

"Nigel!" he said breathlessly. "It's—it's you!"

"Hullo, old thing," said Nigel.

"Hullo. I've been thinking. Look here, I believe they'll get me for this. Last night I couldn't think of anything, except how he looked when he fell, and then later—when it was getting light, you know—I began to see what would happen. I'll be arrested for murder. And I won't be able to prove anything. It'll mean—being hanged."

"Oh, shut your silly face up," implored Nigel. "Why the devil should they think you did it. Don't be fatuous."

"I know why he asked me all that stuff. He thinks I planted the cartridges."

"He damn' well doesn't. He's on an entirely different tack, and it's about that I've come to see you."

"I'm sorry." Gardener dropped into a chair and pressed his hand over his eyes. "I'm making an ass of myself. Fire away."

"Do you remember the Jacob Saint libel case?"

Gardener stared.

"It's funny you should ask that. I suddenly thought of it a little while ago."

"That's good. Think again. Did you know Surbonadier then?"

"He was sent down soon after I went to Cambridge, and we were at different colleges. His real name was Simes. Yes, I'd met him."

"Did you ever think he wrote the article in the *Morning Express* that Saint brought the case about?"

"I'm afraid I'm rather vague about it now, but I remember hearing third-year men talk about it at the time."

"Well, the article was sent in by an unknown writer purporting to be one of the 'Mex' staff. It came from Mossburn, near Cambridge."

"I remember, now." Gardener paused for a moment. "I should think it most unlikely Surbonadier wrote it. He'd hardly want to kill the goose that laid the golden eggs."

"He was supposed to be on bad terms with his uncle."

"Yes, that's true. I remember hearing it. He was a most unaccountable chap, and subject to fits of the vilest sort of temper."

"Why was he sent down?"

"On several accounts. A woman. And then he was mixed up with a drug-taking set. Fearful scandal."

"Drugs, eh?"

"Yes. When Saint found out, he threatened to cut him off altogether. He survived that, and went down for

97

good over some affair with a farmer's daughter, I imagine. Oh, Lord, what's the good of all this?"

"Can't you see? If he wrote that article it's quite possible he's been blackmailing Saint for years."

"You mean Saint—oh no."

"Somebody did it."

"I'm half inclined to think he did it himself. He'd have loved to send me to the gallows." Gardener looked as though he forced himself to say this for the sheer horror of hearing the words. He reminded Nigel of a child opening the pages of a book that he knew would terrify him.

"Do get that idea out of your head, Felix. You're the last man they're thinking of," he declared, and hoped he spoke the truth. "Can you remember the names of any men who were friendly with Surbonadier then?"

"There was a fearful swine called—what was his name?—oh, Gaynor. I can't think of anyone else. He was killed in an aeroplane accident, I believe."

"Not much good. If you remember anything more let me know. I'll go now, and do, for the love of Mike, pull yourself together, old thing."

"I'll try. Good-bye, Nigel."

"Good-bye. Don't ring, I'll let myself out."

Gardener walked to the door and opened it. Nigel paused to collect his cigarette-case, which had slipped into a crevice of his chair. That was why Stephanie Vaughan didn't see him as she came to the door.

"Felix," she said, "I had to see you. You must help me. If they ask you about——"

"Do you remember Nigel Bathgate?" said Gardener.

She saw Nigel then, and couldn't speak. He walked past her and downstairs without uttering another word.

Chapter XII

SURBONADIER'S FLAT

Big Ben struck twelve noon as Nigel made his way back to Scotland Yard. Chief Detective-Inspector Alleyn was engaged, but Nigel was invited to take a seat in the passage outside his room. Presently the door opened and a roaring noise informed him of the presence of Mr. Jacob Saint.

"That's all I know. You can ferret round till you're blue in the face, but you won't find anything else. I'm a plain man, inspector——"

"Oh, I don't think so at all, Mr. Saint," Alleyn said politely.

"And your comedy stuff makes me tired. It's a suicide case. When's the inquest?"

"To-morrow at eleven."

Mr. Saint uttered a rumbling sound and walked out into the passage. He stared at Nigel, failed to recognise him, and made off in the direction of the stairs.

"Hullo, Bathgate," said Alleyn from the doorway. "Come in."

Nigel, by dint of terrific self-suppression, managed to report Wakeford with a certain air of nonchalance. Alleyn listened attentively.

"Wakeford's theory is possible," he said. "Surbonadier was a peculiar individual. He may have written the article, fathered it on to Wakeford, and hugged himself with the thought that he was dealing a sly blow at Uncle Jacob. We know he tried to blackmail him a week or so ago. It's not as inconsistent as it seems."

"Saint himself swore he didn't do it—at the time of the trial, I mean."

"Of course he did. If his nephew had proved to be the author, he would have seemed a better authority

99

than a reporter eager for sensational copy. No—in a way it's a reasonable theory."

"You sound doubtful."

"I am."

"So's Gardener. He doesn't think Surbonadier did it."

"What? You've seen him?"

"Yes. He's got the wind up now and thinks you're going to pull him in."

"He doesn't think Surbonadier wrote the article?"

"He said so, quite honestly, though I'm sure he understood how the theory would point to Saint rather than to himself. All the same, I got the feeling he really believed there might be something in it."

"Tell me exactly what was said."

Nigel repeated, as closely as he could, his conversation with Gardener. Rather reluctantly he described Miss Vaughan's appearance and her unfinished sentence.

"What was she going to warn him about?" he wondered.

"Can't you guess?" Alleyn asked.

"No, I can *not*."

"Think. Think. Think."

"Oh, shut up," said Nigel crossly. "You talk like a Thorndyke."

"Why not? I wish I could sleuth like one. I'll have to have a stab at it, too. Dig up some old dirt at Cambridge."

"Do you think there's anything in the suicide theory?"

"No. He hadn't the guts. I suppose you realise the significance of Gardener's information about the drug coterie at Cambridge?"

"It suggests that Surbonadier might be ' in the know ' that way as well as any other, about his uncle's goings on," said Nigel confusedly.

"I must go," said Alleyn, looking at his watch.

"Where to?"

"The deceased's flat."

"May I come, too?"

"You? I don't know. You're rather a prejudiced party in this case."

" You mean about Felix?"

" Yes. If you come you'll have to give me your word you'll keep quiet about it."

" I will, I swear."

" Not a word to anyone. Nor with arms encumbered thus or this head-shake, or by pronouncing of some doubtful phrase——"

" No—no—no."

" Swear!"

" I swear."

" All right. Let's have lunch and go."

They lunched together at Alleyn's flat, and, after a liqueur and a cigarette, made their way to Surbonadier's rooms in Gerald's Row. A police constable was on guard there and produced the keys. At the door Alleyn turned to Nigel.

" I've little idea," he said, " what we shall find in here. It's an ugly case. Are you sure you wouldn't rather keep out of it?"

" How you do go on," said Nigel. " I'm in on the deal."

" So be it. Here we go." He unlocked the door and they walked in.

The flat comprised four rooms and a bathroom and kitchenette, all opening on the right from a passage that ran their length. The first was Surbonadier's bedroom and the second a sitting-room with folding doors leading to a small dining-room. The kitchenette and bathroom came next and another bedroom at the end. This seemed to be unused, and was filled with trunks, boxes, and odds and ends of furniture. The flats were served by a married couple and their son, who all lived in the basement. Alleyn, after a glance at the small bedroom, sighed and rang up the Yard, suggesting that Inspector Fox or Detective Bailey should come and help. The sitting-room was luxuriously and rather floridly furnished. A framed supplement from *La Vie Parisienne* was a striking note above the sideboard. The cushions, of which there were many, were orange and purple. Alleyn sniffed distastefully.

" May as well begin in here," he said. " He *would* have a satinwood desk, wouldn't he? Disgusting object."

He produced a bunch of keys, selected one, and fitted it in the lock.

"Are those his keys?" asked Nigel.

"They are indeed."

The lock clicked and Alleyn let down the front of the desk. A conglomerate welter of paper fell forward and spilled on to the floor.

"Oh, Lord! Come on, Bathgate. Bills in one pile, receipts in another. Circulars here. Letters there. Read everything and tell me if you strike anything interesting. Wait a moment. You'd better hand over all private letters to me. Here we go. Try and get the bills into chronological order will you?"

There were a great many bills, and the separate accounts had been sent in a great many times, with added reminders that began obsequiously and worked their way through the humble, the plaintive, the reproachful, and the exasperated tenor, until they reached the final and threatening note that indicates "Immediate proceedings." These, however, never appeared to eventuate, and after half an hour's work Nigel made a discovery.

"I say, Alleyn," he said. "He paid all his bills about a year ago, when the shops threatened to dun him, and, as far as I can see, he hasn't paid one since, and they're all threatening to dun him again! I suppose old Saint must have made him a yearly allowance!"

"Old Saint says he made Surbonadier no allowance. He cleared up his debts at Cambridge, gave him a start on the stage, and intimated it was up to little Arthur."

"Really? Well, he was evidently expecting something to come in as far as one can judge by the letters from the shops."

"What did the total of his last pay-out amount to?"

"Wait a bit."

Nigel did some feverish sums, swore under his breath, began again, and finally said, triumphantly:

"Two thousand pounds. That's what he paid out last May and he owes about the same amount again now."

"What's that you've got?" asked Alleyn.

"It's his pass-book. He's overdrawn. Let me see now.

May, last year. There's no note of any large sum to his credit. It must have been cash. No, by Jove—here it is. Two thousand paid in on the twenty-fifth of May last year."

"I see," said Alleyn thoughtfully. "I see."

"Doesn't that look like blackmail money?"

"It does."

"From Saint. I bet it was from Saint."

"Maybe."

"You sound dubious."

"I am. Here's old Fox."

Inspector Fox heard the news without enthusiasm.

"He's still wedded to Props," said Alleyn. "Let's get on with the horrid job."

"Deceased seems to have kept every letter that was ever sent to him," said Fox. "Here's a little pile from somebody called Steff."

"Steff?" echoed Alleyn sharply. "Let me see."

He took the letters and walked to the window with them. He stood very still, glancing swiftly at page after page, and placing each face downwards on the sill as he finished it.

"A pig of a man," he said suddenly.

"That's what Felix called him," remarked Nigel.

"So she told me."

"She?"

"Stephanie—Vaughan."

"Steff—oh, I see," said Nigel eagerly. "The letters are from her."

"Oh, Lord," said Alleyn, looking at him wearily, "you're there, are you?"

"Is there anything useful, sir?" asked Fox.

"There's a good deal that's painful. They start off in her best leading-lady manner—all ecstasy and style, and fashionable dalliance. Then he must have shown up in his true colours. She is horrified by something, but still rather mannered and flowery. She keeps it up until about a week—no—two days ago. Then there are two little notes. 'Please let's stop, Arthur. I'm sorry. I can't help it if I've changed,' and the signature. That was written two days ago. The last, which is in a different key, was actually sent yesterday morning."

"Carrying on with him and Mr. Gardener together, seemingly," said Fox; "but I don't see that it helps."

"I'm afraid it does help a little," Alleyn rejoined. "Ah well—on with the hunt."

At last the contents of the desk were exhausted, and Alleyn led them to the spare bedroom, where the search began again and went on wearily. The Yard men were terribly thorough. Finally they unearthed an old trunk that had been put away in the wardrobe. Nigel switched the lights on and drew the curtains. It was already beginning to get dark in the room. Alleyn opened the trunk. Here they found letters from a great many women, but beyond throwing a little extra light on Mr. Surbonadier's unsavoury character, they were of no value.

At the bottom were two old newspapers, carefully folded. Alleyn pounced on one, shook it open, and folded it back. Fox and Nigel looked over his shoulder and read in flaring capitals and single word "Cocaine!" and underneath : "Amazing revelation of the illicit drug trade. Fool's Paradise—and after."

The paper was the *Morning Express* of March, 1929.

"The story itself!" shouted Nigel. "Look, Alleyn, look! And there's Wakeford's signature, reproduced across the top."

"Was that done with all his articles?"

"I think so. All the middle-page, special articles. The 'Mex' always did it."

"It's quite a clear-cut reproduction," said Alleyn. "Good enough to forge from, any day. And an easy one to copy, too."

"Of course," said Fox slowly, "the deceased would be interested even if he had no hand in the matter."

"Quite so," agreed Alleyn absently. He read some of the letterpress. "It certainly points very directly at Saint," he said. "There's another paper left. That will be the account of the libel action."

"You're quite right, sir—it is."

"Yes. Well, now we turn to little Arthur's bedroom.

We are looking for a small strong box. Perhaps a cash box. What are you staring at, Bathgate?"

"You," said Nigel simply.

The bedroom was extremely ornate, and smelt of stale incense. "*Quite* disgusting," muttered Alleyn, and opened a window. They set to work again, leaving Fox to deal with the bathroom. He made the first discovery—a hypodermic syringe in the cuboard above the basin. Nigel found another in the bedside-table drawer, and with it a little oblong packet.

"Dope," said Alleyn. "I thought he was still at it. Let me see." He examined the packet closely. "It's the same as the lot we got from Sniffy Quarles," he said. " 'Oh, what a tangled web we weave when first we practise to deceive.' "

"That's right," said Inspector Fox, and returned to the bathroom.

"I adore Fox," said Alleyn. "He's the perfect embodiment, the last loveliest expression, of horse sense. There is nothing in this chest of drawers, nor in any of the pockets of Mr. Surbonadier's suits, except—hullo, what's this?"

It was another letter, this time a very humble affair written on common paper. Alleyn handed it to Nigel who read:

"Dear Mr. Surbonadier, please don't take no more notice of me because I'm sorry about what I done and Dad's that angry he found out and Bert is a decent fellow so I told him, and he's forgiven me but if you ever look at me agen he says he will do for you so please do not look at me and oblige yours sincerly Trixie. p.s. I said nothing about getting them little parcels but will not get any more T."

"Who's Bert?" asked Nigel.

"Albert Hickson is the property master's name," said Alleyn.

"One up to Fox," said Nigel.

"He'll think so—yes. So Trixie got it for him. I must . see Trixie again."

He got a chair, put it by the wardrobe and stood on it. Then he reached up and groped at the back of the top shelf.

"Stand by!" he said suddenly.

Nigel hurried to his side. From behind a leather hat box Alleyn drew out a small tin, very sturdily made, and bound with iron.

"That's what we're looking for," he said.

Chapter XIII

CONTENTS OF AN IRON-BOUND BOX

"How the devil did you know he had this?" asked Nigel.

Alleyn climbed down from his perch, put his hand in his pocket and produced a small key hanging on a long very fine, steel chain.

"We found this round his neck. It suggested something of the sort to me. These boxes are made by one particular firm and the keys are rather individual. Now let us open it."

He inserted the little key and turned it twice. The lock gave a sharp click and opened. Alleyn lifted the lid.

"More paper," said Nigel.

"Yes. Wait a moment."

Alleyn put the box down on the glass top of the dressing-table. From his pocket he took two pairs of tweezers and, using them delicately, lifted out a sheet of blue notepaper. It was folded. He opened it up carefully, and bent over it. Nigel heard him draw in his breath.

"Don't touch it," he said, "but look."

And Nigel looked. On the paper two words were written over and over again:

"Edward Wakeford. Edward Wakeford. Edward Wakeford."

Without a word Alleyn went out of the room, returning

followed by Fox, with the newspaper they had found in the trunk. He folded down the heading of the special article and laid it beside the paper on the dressing-table. The writing of the signature was indentical.

"Why, in Heaven's name, did he keep it?" whispered Nigel.

"You may well ask," said Fox. "Human nature's very rum, sir, very rum indeed. Vanity, as like as not."

"*Vanitas vanitatum,*" Alleyn murmured. "But not this time, Fox."

The second paper proved to be another letter. It was signed H.J.M., and began: "Dear Mr. Saint."

"Hullo!" said Alleyn. "Here's the ex-footman coming out in a blaze of dubious glory. He mentioned this. It's from Mortlake. 'Please find enclosed my cheque for five hundred pounds in settlement of our little debt. The goods have all been disposed of, as per arrangement. The trade in shantung silk is particularly satisfactory, but I have great hopes of celanese next June when our Mr. Charles comes over. Yours faithfully——' Oh, joy, oh rapture, my Foxkin, this is Mortlake himself! It's a relic of our last little catch. Do you remember? Please to remember, my Fox."

"I remember all right. Shantung was heroin and celanese was cocaine. We rounded 'em all up except Mortlake."

"And 'our Mr. Charles' was none other than Sniffy Quarles, who got five of the best, bless his little soul. This will just about settle Mr. Mortlake. So *that's* what Surbonadier had had up his sleeve for Jacob Saint."

"Well, sir, I must say it begins to look more as if Saint's our man. Although you've got to admit Trixie's letter still points my way."

"Aren't you both excited?" Nigel observed perkily.

"You must allow us our drab thrills. There's nothing more in the box."

Alleyn refolded the papers, using the utmost care not to touch the surfaces. He put them in a black japanned case that Fox produced. Then he shut the iron-bound box, returned it to the wardrobe shelf, and lit a cigarette.

"Bailey had better get to work on the papers," he said. "There's nothing else here. I'm going to call on Miss Vaughan. No. Wait a moment. I think I'll ring her up."

He sat on the bed, nursing his foot and rocking backwards and forwards. An expression of extreme distaste crossed his face. He took up the telephone directory, consulted it, and with a fastidious lift of his shoulders, dialled a number on the bedside telephone. The others waited.

"Is that Miss Stephanie Vaughan's flat? May I speak to her? Will you say it's Mr. Roderick Alleyn? Thank you.

A pause. Alleyn traced his finger slowly round the base of the telephone.

"Is that Miss Vaughan? Please forgive me for bothering you. I am ringing up from Surbonadier's flat. We intended to go through his papers this afternoon, but I find it's going to be a very big job. There are some letters." He paused. "Yes. I realise it is very disagreeable and I think it would be easiest for you if you could meet me here, and should there be any questions I can ask them straight away. That is extremely kind of you. I am locking the place up now and leaving it, but I thought of returning about nine this evening? Could you come then? May I pick you up? Oh, I see. At nine o'clock, then. Good-bye." He hung up the receiver. "What's the time?" he asked.

"Five o'clock," said Nigel.

"Fox—will you take the papers back to the Yard and let Bailey have them? And tell the constable outside he can go."

"Go!" echoed Fox dazedly.

"Yes, and don't send anyone to relieve him. I'm staying on here myself."

"Until nine?" asked.

"Until nine—or earlier."

"Yes," said Alleyn. "You can get hold of Felix Gardener again. You can tell him the police believe Surbonadier to have written the article in the *Morning Express*. Ask him if he can give us more information about Surbonadier's Cambridge days. Anything at all that he can remember. There may be something he's holding back. He's feeling jumpy, you tell me. If he's got the idea we're suspecting him his natural reaction will be to disclaim any previous relationship with Surbonadier."

Nigel looked uncomfortable.

" I don't like the idea of pumping him

" Then you are useless. I'll see him myself."

" Sorry if I'm tiresome."

" All amateurs are tiresome. You want to be in on this, but you shy off anything that is at all unpleasant. We had this out before in the Wilde case. You'd much better keep out of it, Bathgate. I should have said so at the beginning."

" If you can assure me Felix is safe——"

" I can give you no assurances about anybody who was behind the scenes. I have my own theory, but it may be all wrong. It's by no means cast-iron and a new development might set us off on a completely new track after any one of them, from Gardener himself down to old Blair. You want me to assure you with my hand on my heart that I am not interested in Gardener. I can't do it. Of course. I'm interested in him. He fired the revolver. I might have arrested him there and then. He's one of the mob, and I've got to prove to myself he didn't plant the cartridges. Like everyone else in the case, he isn't volunteering information. As an innocent man he's a fool if he tries to blind the police. He may have a specific reason for doing so. He's in love. Think that out. If you choose, you may tell him the theory as regards Saint, and if he knows anything about Surbonadier's past that may throw light on that theory, and cares to tell you, and you are still on the side of justice—well and good. Otherwise I shall have to ask you to regard me as you would any other detective on his job, and to expect to get no information but the sort of stuff you can publish in your paper. Have I made myself intelligible?"

"Abundantly. I can take a snub with as good a grace as anyone else, I hope," said Nigel miserably.

"I'm sorry you look at it like that. What line do you mean to take?"

"May I think it over? If I decide to pull out, you may be quite sure I shall treat this afternoon's discoveries as entirely confidential. I promised that, anyway. And I'll let you see my copy, of course."

"That's a very fair answer. Let me know at my flat this evening, will you? Now I must ask you both to go."

Nigel followed Fox into the passage. At the door he turned and looked back.

"Well—good-bye for the present," he muttered.

"Good-bye you old sausage," said Inspector Alleyn.

Fox told the constable at the entrance to the flat to go off. Then he turned to the still discomfited Nigel.

"I dare say you think the Chief's been a bit hard, sir," he ventured, "but you don't want to look at it that way. It's a matter of what you might call professional etiquette. The Chief likes you, you see, and he's so—so blasted honest, if you'll excuse me. His job has to come before anything. Don't you worry about Mr. Gardener. He's been the cat's-paw, and nothing else, and if he starts holding back information he's very foolish."

"I don't think he has done anything of the sort," complained Nigel.

"Well, all the better. If you decide to help us, Mr. Bathgate, I'm sure you won't regret it and I'm sure Chief Inspector Alleyn will be very pleased."

Nigel looked at his large, comfortable face and suddenly liked him very much.

"It's nice of you to bother, inspector," he said. "I was a bit disgruntled. He made me feel such an ass and—and I do admire him so very much."

"You're not alone in that, sir. Well, I must be off. Going my way, sir?"

"I'm for Chester Terrace."

"And I'm for the Yard. No rest for the wicked. Good night, sir."

"Good night, inspector."

Nigel's flat in Chester Terrace was a short walk from Gerald's Row. He strode along quickly, still rather miserable over his lecture from Alleyn. He had only gone a couple of hundred yards when a taxi passed him, moving slowly along the kerb as though cruising for a passenger. Nigel automatically shook his head, and then saw that the man had a fare—a woman. As the cab passed him a streamer of light from the street lamp caught her face. It was Stephanie Vaughan. She gave no hint of recognition, and in a moment had passed him. He turned and stared after the taxi. She must have misunderstood, he thought, and is going now to the flat. However, the man drove slowly down the little street, past Surbonadier's windows, and then turned off to the left and disappeared.

"Rum!" thought Nigel and walked on thoughtfully. "Very rum!" he said aloud.

Back in his own flat he turned on the light and, after further cogitation, decided to try and put himself in a better mood by writing to Angela North, who does not come into this story. She was an ardent admirer of Chief Detective-Inspector Alleyn and would know just how raw Nigel felt. Would she suggest he kept in the game? Would she tell him his scruples about "pumping" Gardener were ridiculous? He couldn't ask her without breaking confidence. Damn it all, what *was* he going to do? Perhaps he'd better go to the Queen's in Cliveden Place and have an evening meal. He wasn't hungry. Alleyn was fed up with him and had made him feel young, and a prig. He knew, Good Lord, that Felix hadn't murdered Arthur Surbonadier. Why shouldn't he ask him if——

The telephone pealed shrilly. Nigel muttered and grumbled and took off the receiver.

Gardener's voice came urgently.

"Is that you, Nigel? Look here, I want to see you. There's something I didn't tell you, about Cambridge, this morning. I was a fool. Could I see you now?"

"Yes," said Nigel. "Yes."

"Will you come here or would you rather I came to you? How about dining here with me? Will you?"

"Yes," said Nigel. "Thank you, Felix."

"Well, don't change—come along now."

"Yes," said Nigel. "Thank you, Felix."

They rang off. He could have shouted with joy. His problem was solved. He rushed to the bathroom and washed, lavishly. He changed his shirt and brushed his hair. Seized with a desire to acquire a little merit in Alleyn's eyes, he rang up Surbonadier's flat. He could hear the telephone ringing there and waited for some time, but nobody answered it. Alleyn had gone, after all. He would ring up again later. He seized his hat and ran downstairs. He hailed a taxi, gave Gardener's address, and flung himself back. Only then did it occur to him that it was very clever of Chief Detective-Inspector Alleyn to have guessed that Gardener would be able to tell them something more about the peculiar behaviour of Arthur Surbonadier, during the days when he was an undergraduate. Gradually he was conscious of an idea that edged in at the back of his mind, an idea that was still only half sensed. He examined it now more closely, letting it come up to the front of his consciousness. For a moment he shied round it nervously, but it was insistent, and presently he fell to reasoning it out with logical persistence. Then a great light dawned on Nigel.

"That's it," he whispered. "That's it. Gosh, what a blind fool I've been." And then with complete understanding he thought: "Poor old Felix!"

Meanwhile in Surbonadier's flat it had grown very dark.

Chapter XIV

GARDENER LOOKS BACKWARDS

"If you don't mind, Nigel," said Gardener, "I'm going to get this off my chest, right away. It'll clear the air. There's a drink. Sit down." He looked less jumpy and nightmare ridden, thought Nigel, and had the air of a man who has come to a decision and is glad of it.

"It's this," he began. "When you came this morning, I was properly under the weather. Hadn't slept a wink and the—the awfulness of having killed Arthur Surbonadier had given place to the terror of being suspected by your friend, Alleyn. You simply can't imagine what that sort of fear is like. Perhaps, if a man's guilty, he is less panic-sticken than I was. It seemed to me I couldn't prove I was *not* guilty, and that, in spite of everything you said, I was the man they really suspected."

"You were quite wrong."

"I hope so. Then, I was sure I was right. Well, I couldn't think of anything coherently, but when you started asking me about the libel case and if I knew Surbonadier at Cambridge I thought: 'He's been sent to ask that. Alleyn thinks I'll be off my guard with Nigel' I can't tell you how awful I felt. No—let me go on. So I half lied. I said I didn't know Arthur well in those days. It wasn't true—I did know him pretty well for a short time—before I realised quite how unpleasant he was. I was younger than he, and perhaps even more of an ass than most youths. I thought it thrillingly daring and sort of 'draining life to the dregs' kind of thing, when he asked me to a heroin party."

"Good Lord!" apostrophised Nigel.

"Yes. I only went once and it was quite beastly. I didn't take nearly as much as the others, and it didn't have a great effect. I probably offered more resistance Next morning I felt I'd made a fool of myself, and I thought I'd make a clean break. So I called on Surbonadier to tell him so. I wanted to put it straight. He was still pretty dopey, and inclined to be maudlin. He began to confide in me. He told me things about his uncle and —and he talked about Stephanie Vaughan." Gardener stopped speaking, hesitated, and then said :

"I'd seen her. She'd come up for a production of *Othello*. If I said I loved her from then onwards, I suppose you'd think it very highfalutin. It's true, though. And when Surbonadier began to tell me how friendly they were, I hated him. Then he said his uncle was going to give her leading parts and he began to tell me how he hated his uncle, and what a lot he knew about him. He told me how Saint was mixed up in the drug trade. He told me about his mistresses. Stephanie seemed so innocent, and when I thought of her in that *galère* it had a terrible effect on me. I was dreadfully young. Saint seemed like the embodiment of all evil. It was nightmarish. I don't understand psychology, and I expect the heroin had something to do with it. We were neither of us normal. Anyway, when Surbonadier told me, in a dopey sort of way, that he could, if he chose, deal his uncle a pretty shrewd blow, I encouraged him feverishly. He said that Saint was refusing to pay his bills, but that he knew too much and could make him. He then suggested writing that article, and I urged him to do it and egged him on. Then I suddenly remembered what I'd come for, and tried to tell him I wouldn't go to any more of his parties. He didn't seem to pay much attention. He was engrossed with the idea of the article. I left him and, from that time on, I had nothing to do with him. When the article came out I guessed who had done it, and once, when we met, he tried to pump me. I told him, shortly enough, that he'd nothing to fear from me and, until to-night, I've never spoken of it."

"What made you decide to tell me?" Nigel asked.

Gardener did not answer immediately. Then he said slowly : "I thought the police would start ferreting round in Surbonadier's past, and would find out I had known him."

"That's not it," said Nigel compassionately. "You thought they were—on another trail altogether. I'm right, aren't I? You realised that unless they knew Surbonadier had been blackmailing Saint, they might suspect someone else altogether. Isn't that it?"

"Then they *are*——?"

"I don't think so. Anyhow, this will clinch it. Surely *she* doesn't think *you* are guilty?"

"Each of us was afraid—— And then this morning when she came in—— My God, they couldn't suspect her."

"You needn't worry about that now, and as for you——"

"Yes—as for me?" Gardener looked at him. "Nigel," he said. "Do you mind telling me this? Do you in your heart of hearts hide a sort of doubt about me? Do you?"

"No. On my word of honour."

"Then, on my word of honour, I'm not guilty of Surbonadier's death and neither is she. There's something I can't tell you, but—we're not guilty."

"I believe you, old thing."

"I feel better," said Felix Gardener. "Let's dine."

The dinner was an excellent one, and the wine extremely good. They talked about many things, sometimes harking back to the case, but now with less sense of restraint. Once Gardener said suddenly:

"It's pretty gruesome to think of the immediate future of—of the Simes family."

"Then don't think of it. What's happening at the Unicorn?"

"You mean about production? Would you believe it, he actually thought of going on with *The Rat and the Beaver*."

"What!"

"Yes, he did. As soon as the police were out of it. Of course I refused to carry on, and so did Stephanie. The others didn't like it, but didn't actually refuse. Then he began to wonder if after all it *would* be a big attraction—with other people playing the leads. The papers might comment unfavourably. So a new piece goes into rehearsal next week."

"What'll you do?"

"Oh, I'll wait. There are other managements." He grimaced wryly. "They tell me I'm a sort of popular figure, and it's helped my publicity. Maudlin sympathy coupled with morbid curiosity, I suppose. Come into the studio room."

They sat down in front of the fire. The front door bell of the flat rang, and Gardener's servant came through with a letter.

"This has just come by special messenger, sir," he said. "There's no answer."

Gardener slit the envelope and drew out a sheet of paper. Nigel lit a cigarette and wandered round the room. He had paused in front of a photograph of Gardener's brother when he was recalled by an exclamation from his host.

"For Heaven's sake," murmured Gardener, "what's all this in aid of?"

He held out the sheet of paper.

It contained a solitary typewritten paragraph, which Nigel read with bewilderment:

"If your job and your life are any use to you, mind your business or you'll lose both. Forget what's past, or you will get worse than a sore foot."

Nigel and Gardener stared at one another in utter bewilderment.

"Coo lumme!" said Nigel at last.

"Not 'alf," agreed Gardener with emphasis.

"Have you got a sore foot?" Nigel inquired.

"Yes, I have. I told you somebody trod on it."

"Somebody who smelt like Jacob Saint?"

"I only thought so. I wasn't sure."

"Look here," said Nigel, "this is no joke. Alleyn ought to know about it."

"Oh, help."

"Well, he ought to, anyway. I'll ring him up, if I may."

"Where will you find him?"

Nigel paused and considered. Possibly Alleyn might not want him to disclose his whereabouts. Nigel did not even know if he would still be at Surbonadier's flat. He looked up the number in the directory and dialled it.

"He may not be at home," he said deceitfully. Again, he could hear the bell pealing in the flat in Gerald's Row. Again there was no answer. He felt vaguely uneasy.

"Nobody there?" said Gardener.

"I could try the Yard," mumbled Nigel. "But I'll leave it for the moment. Let's have another squint at that paper."

He and Gardener spent the next hour in speculation on the authorship of the letter. Gardener said he didn't think Saint would do it. Nigel said if he was rattled, there was no knowing what he would do.

"If he's a murderer——" he began.

"I'm not sure that he is. Another view is that he's scared I may know something of what Surbonadier found out about him, and thinks I may do exactly what I have done—come clean."

"Did he know you were friendly with Surbonadier?"

"Yes, Arthur introduced us in those days. Afterwards, when I took to the boards, he saw me in the first decent part I played, and remembered me. That's partly how I got my first shop under his management. Not nice to think of now. Arthur resented it very much. He used to tell people I'd got in on his family ticket. God, what a dirty game it is! Do you remember what I said about actors?"

"I do."

"Look at the way they behaved last night, with Surbonadier lying dead on the stage. All of them acting their socks off—except Stephanie."

Nigel looked at him curiously. He seemed to hear Alleyn's sardonic "Lovely exit, wasn't it?" after Miss Vaughan had left the stage. He remembered the curiously seductive note she struck afterwards, in her interview with the inspector. Even he, Alleyn, had stood longer than was necessary with his hand on her bruised shoulder. Nigel thought virtuously of his Angela and felt a little superior.

"I wonder what she's doing?" Gardener said presently. "I wanted to go and see her to-night, but she said she'd ring up."

"What's she so frightened about?" Nigel blurted out. Gardener's face whitened. The look that had been there that morning returned.

"Of course she's frightened," he said at last. "She thinks Alleyn realised Surbonadier was pestering her and threatening her. It wasn't hard last night to see how the land lay. She always made nothing of it to me. Until this morning I didn't realise myself what he was up to. This morning she showed me her shoulder, and told me that after I left her he struck her—the swine! My God, if I'd known that!"

"It's damn' lucky for you that you didn't," said Nigel. "And he's dead now, Felix."

"She told me Alleyn had seen the bruise. She thought Alleyn suspected her. She's terribly highly strung and the shock has been almost overwhelming."

"And you were afraid for her, too?"

"Yes—after this morning. Until then, selfish imbecile that I was, I thought only of myself. That they should even think of her! It's monstrous."

"Well, don't worry. I haven't heard one of them ever hint it. I tell you they are off on different tacks. I'd be breaking confidence if I said more than that. And now, if you don't mind, Felix, I'll be off. It was a devilish late night last night and you look as if you wanted sleep too. Take a couple of aspirins and a peg and leave off worrying. Good night."

"Good night, Nigel. We've never known each other particularly well, but I hope we may from now on. I'm rather grateful to you."

"Bosh. Good night."

It was half-past ten when Nigel got back to Chester Terrace, and he was, he discovered, dead tired. He had, however, a story to write for to-morrow, and he didn't want to leave it till the morning.

Very wearily he sat down to his typewriter and ran in a sheet of paper. He thought for a moment and then began to tap at the keys:

THE UNICORN MURDER

FRESH DEVELOPMENTS
SAINT LIBEL CASE RECALLED

As he worked his thoughts kept turning to Alleyn. The inspector ought to know about Felix. At last he reached out his hand and took up the telephone. Surely by this time Alleyn would be home. He dialled the number of his flat, rested his head on his hand and waited.

Chapter XV

ACHILLES' HEEL

After Nigel and Inspector Fox had gone out of the room, and the door was shut, Inspector Alleyn stood very still and listened to their footsteps dying away down the passage. He heard Fox speak to the constable at the entrance door, and a little later their voices floated up from the footpath beneath.

If an onlooker had been there, he might perhaps have supposed Alleyn's thoughts were unpleasant ones. The inspector had the type of face that is sometimes described as "winged." The corners of his mouth made two deep depressions such as a painter will render with a crisp upward stroke of the brush. His nostrils, too, slanted up, and so did the outside corners of his very dark eyebrows. It was an attractive and fastidious face and, when nobody watched him, a very expressive one. At the moment it suggested extreme distaste. One might have guessed that he had just done something that was repugnant to him, or that he was about to undertake a task which displeased him.

Alleyn looked at his watch, sighed, turned out the lights, and went to the window, where he was careful to stand behind the curtains. From here he could watch, unseen, the desultory traffic of Gerald's Row. Perhaps only two minutes had passed since Nigel and Fox had gone. A solitary taxi came very slowly down the little street. It loitered past the flat. He had an aeroplane view of it, but he fancied that the occupant's face was in an unusual and uncomfortable position, below the window, for all the world as though its owner were kneeling on the floor, enjoying a worm's-eye view of the flat, and taking rather particular care not to be seen. At this Inspector Alleyn smiled sideways. He was trying to remember the exact location of the nearest telephone booth. The taxi disappeared and he moved away from the window, took out his cigarette-case, thought better of it, and pocketed it again. Three of four minutes passed. His meditations were uncannily checked by the bedside telephone, which came to life abruptly with a piercing double ring. Alleyn smiled rather more broadly, and sat on the bed with his hands in his pockets. The telephone rang twenty times and then inconsequently went dead. He returned to the window. It was now very quiet in the street, so that when someone came briskly on foot from Elizabeth Street, he heard the steps a long way off. Suddenly he drew back from the window, and with a very desolate groan, crawled under the bed, which was a low one. He was obliged to lie flat on his front. He rearranged the valance, which he had noted disgustedly was of rose-coloured taffeta. Then he lay perfectly still.

Presently a key turned in the entrance door to the flat, and whoever it was who came in must have taken off their shoes, because only the faintest sound, a kind of sensation of movement, told him someone was coming, step by stealthy step, along the passage. Then he heard the handle of the door turn and from under the edge of the valance, in the dim light reflected from the street lamps, he saw the door itself swing slowly open. In the shadow beyond a darker shadow moved forward. The faintest rustle told him that someone had come into the room. Another rustle and the scaly sound of curtain rings. The light from the street was blotted out. When the silence had become intolerable, the telephone above him rang out again shrilly. The bell pealed on and on. The bed above him sank down and touched his shoulders stealthily. The noise of the telephone changed into a stupidly coarse clatter. Something had been pressed down over it. Alleyn counted twenty more double rings before it stopped.

Nigel over in Chester Terrace had hung up his receiver and gone to dine with Gardener.

A faint sigh of relief sounded above Alleyn's head. He could have echoed it with heartfelt enthusiasm when the bed rustled again and the weight on his shoulders was lifted. Next came the sound of chair legs, dragging a little on the carpet, and coming down finally across the room. The wardrobe door creaked. A pause, followed by furtive scrabblings. Then a metallic click. Alleyn cleared his throat.

" You'll simply have to turn up the light, Miss Vaughan," he said.

She didn't scream, but he knew how near she came to it by the desperate little gasp she gave. Then she whispered bravely :

" Who is it?"

" The Law," said Alleyn grandly.

" You !"

" Yes. Do turn the light on. There's no reason at all why you shouldn't. The switch is just inside the door." He sneezed violently. " Bless you, Mr. Alleyn," he said piously.

The room was flooded with pink light. Alleyn had thrust his head and shoulders out from the end of the bed.

She stood with one hand still on the switch. In the other she carried the little iron-bound box. Her eyes were dilated like those of a terrified child. She looked fantastically beautiful.

Alleyn wriggled out and stood up.

"I think bed dust is quite the beastliest kind of dust there is," he complained.

Her fingers slid away from the door handle. Her figure slackened. As she pitched forward he caught her. The box fell with a clatter to the floor.

"No, no," he said. "This won't do. You're not a woman who faints when she meets a reverse. You, with your iron nerve. You haven't fainted. Your heart beats steadily."

"Yours, on the contrary," she whispered, "Is hammering violently."

He put her on her feet and held her elbows.

"Sit down," he said curtly.

She pulled herself away, and sat in the arm-chair he lugged forward.

"All the same," said Miss Vaughan, "you did give me a fright." She looked at him very steadily. "What a fool I've been. Such an obvious trap."

"I was surprised that it caught you. When I saw you in the taxi, I knew I had succeeded, and then a little later, when you rang— I *thought* Surbonadier would have given you a latch-key."

"I had meant to return it."

"Really? I must say. I can't think where the attraction lay. Evidently you are a bad selector."

"Not always."

"Perhaps not always."

"After all, you have nothing against me. Why shouldn't I come here? You yourself suggested it."

"At nine, with me. What were you looking for in that box?"

"My letters," she said quickly. "I wanted to destroy them."

"They are not there."

"Then like Ophelia I was the more deceived."

"You weren't deceived," he said bitterly.

"Mr. Alleyn—give me my letters. If I give you my word, my solemn word, that they had nothing whatever to do with his death——"

"I've read them."

She turned very white.

"All of them?"

"Yes. Even yesterday's note."

"What are you going to do—arrest me? You are alone here."

"I do not think you would struggle and make a scene. I can't picture myself dragging you, dishevelled and breathless, into the street, and blowing a fanfare on my police whistle while you lacerated my face with your nails.

"No, that would be too undignified."

She began to weep, not noisily or with ugly distortions of her face, but beautifully. Her eyes flooded and then overflowed. She held her handkerchief over them for a moment.

"I'm cold," she said.

He took the eiderdown cover off the bed and gave it to her. It slipped out of her hands and she looked at him helplessly. He put it round her, tucking it into the chair. Suddenly she seized the collar of his coat.

"Look at me!" said Stephanie Vaughan. "Look at me. Do I look like a murderess?"

He took her wrists and tried to pull them down, but she clung to his coat.

"I promise you I didn't mean what I said in that letter. I wanted to frighten him. He threatened me. I only wanted to frighten him."

He wrenched her hands away, and straightened himself.

"You've hurt me," she said.

"You obliged me to. We'd better not prolong this business."

"At least let me explain myself. If, after you've heard me, you still think I'm guilty, I'll go with you without another word."

"I must warn you——"

"I know. But I must speak. Sit down for five minutes and listen to me. I won't bolt. Lock the door, if you like."

"Very well."

He locked the door and pocketed the key. Then he sat on the end of the bed, and waited.

"I've known Arthur Surbonadier for six years," she said at last. "I went to Cambridge to take part in a charity show that was being got up by some of the under-graduates. They engaged me to play Desdemona. I was a novice, then, and very young. Arthur was good-looking in those days and he always had a charm for women. I don't expect you to understand that. He introduced me to Felix, but I hardly remembered Felix when we met again. He had never forgotten me, he says. Arthur was attracted to me. He introduced me to Jacob Saint, and through that I got a real start in my profession. We were both given parts in a Saint show that was produced at the end of the year. He was passionately in love with me. That doesn't begin to express it. He was completely and utterly absorbed as though, apart from me, he had no reality. I was fascinated and—and so it happened. He asked me over and over again to marry him, but I didn't want to get married, and I soon knew he was a rotter. He told me about all sorts of things he had done. He had a fantastic hatred of his uncle, and once, at Cambridge, he wrote an article that attributed all sorts of things to Saint. There was a case about it—I expect you remember—but Saint never thought Arthur had done it, because Arthur was so dependent on him. He told me all about that and his own vices. He still attracted me. Then I met Felix and——" She made a little gesture with her hands, a gesture that he might have recognised as one of her stage tricks.

"From that time onwards, I wanted to break off my relationship with Arthur. He terrified me, and he threatened to tell Felix about—all sorts of things." She paused, and a different note came into her voice. "Felix," she said, was a different type. He belongs to another caste. In a funny sort of way he's intolerant. But—he's dreadfully honourable. If Arthur had told him! I was terrified. I began to write those letters, at the time I went to New York, but when I got back Arthur still dominated me.

Yesterday—it seems years ago—he came to see me, and there was a scene. I thought I would try to frighten him and, after he left, I wrote that note."

"In which you said: 'If you don't promise to-night to let me go I'll put you out of it altogether.'"

"My God, I meant I'd tell Saint what he'd done—how he'd written that article!"

"He's been blackmailing Saint for years. Surely you knew that?"

She looked as if she was thunderstruck.

"Did you know?" asked Alleyn.

"No. He never told me that."

"I see," said Alleyn.

She looked piteously at him. She was rubbing her wrists where he had gripped them. As if on an impulse, she held out her hand.

"Can't you believe me—and pity me?" she whispered.

A silence fell between them. For some seconds neither moved or spoke, and then he was beside her, her hand held close between both of his. He raised it, her fingers threaded through his own. He had bent his head and stood in what seemed to be a posture of profound meditation.

"You've won," he said at last.

She leant forward and touched her face against his fingers, and then, with her free hand, she pulled aside the eiderdown quilt and let it slide to the floor.

"Last night I thought you were going to kiss my hand," she said.

"To-night——" He kissed it deliberately. In the silence that followed they heard someone come at a brisk walk down the narrow street. The sound of footsteps seemed to bring her back to earth. She drew her hand away and stood up.

"I congratulate you," she said.

"On what?"

"On your intelligence. You would have made a bad gaffe if you had arrested me. Will you let me go away now?"

" If you must."

" Indeed I must. Tell me—what made you first suspect me?"

" Your cosmetic was on the cartridges."

She turned away to the window and looked into the street.

" But how extraordinary," she said quietly. " That bottle was overturned on my table. Arthur himself knocked it over." She seemed to ponder this for a moment and then she said quickly : " That means whoever did it was in my room?"

" Yes. Your room was empty just before it happened. You were talking to Gardener next door."

" No, no. That's all wrong. At least he *may* have gone in there. No, he didn't. He was on the stage by that time. Arthur knocked the bottle over. He was splashed with the stuff. When he put the cartridges in the drawer, there was some on his hands. Probably there was still some more of it on his thumb when he loaded the revolver. He realised it was all up with him, and he wanted Felix accused of murder. Or me. He may have deliberately used my wet-white. It would have been like him."

" Would it? You poor child !"

" Yes. Oh, I *know* that's it."

" I wonder if you can be right," said Alleyn.

" I'm sure I am."

" I'll approach it again from that angle," he said, but he scarcely seemed aware of what he said. He looked at her hungrily, as though he would never be satisfied with looking.

" I must go now. May I take—the letters—or must they come out?"

" You may have them."

He went into the next room and got the letters. When he came back with them she looked them through carefully.

" But there's one missing," she said.

" I don't think so."

" Indeed, there is. Are you sure you didn't drop it?"

" Those are all we found."

She looked distractedly round the room.

" I must find it," she insisted. " It must be somewhere here. He threatened to show that one, in particular, to Felix."

" We sifted everything. He must have burnt it."

" No, no. I'm sure he didn't. Please let me look. I know where he kept all his things." She hunted frantically through all the rooms. Once she stopped and looked at him.

" You wouldn't——?"

" I have held back none of your letters, on my word of honour."

" Forgive me," she said, and fell to hunting again. At last she confessed herself defeated.

" If it's found you shall have it," Alleyn assured her. She thanked him, but was clearly not satisfied. At last he persuaded her to stop hunting.

" I'll telephone for a taxi," he said.

" No, don't do that. I'll walk to the corner and get one. I'd rather."

" I'll come with you. I've just to lock up."

" No. We'll say good night now," she laughed. " I can't be seen out with you—you're too compromising."

"Nous avons changé tout cela."

" You think so, do you, inspector? Good night."

" Good night, Stephanie. If I weren't a policeman——"

" Yes?"

" Give me that key, madam."

" Oh ! The key of the flat. Where did I put it? Now that's lost."

" Is it on the chain?"

He pulled at the chain round her neck, found the key, which had been hidden under her dress, and slipped it off. This brought them close together, and he saw she was trembling.

" You are quite done up," he said. " Shan't I come with you? Give me that pleasure."

" No, please. Good night again."

He touched her hand.

" Good night."

She took a step towards him, looked into his eyes, and smiled. In a moment he had her close-held in his arms.

"What's this?" he said roughly. "I know you're everything I most deplore—and yet—look at this. Shall I kiss you?"

"Why not?"

"Every reason why not."

"How strangely you look at me. As if you were examining my face inch by inch."

He released her suddenly.

"Please go," he said.

In a moment she had gone. He leaned from the window and watched her come out on to the pavement below. She turned towards South Eaton Place. A few seconds later, a man came out of an alley-way by the flat, paused to light a cigarette, and then strolled off in the same direction.

Alleyn closed the window carefully and put out the light. In walking to the door he stubbed his toe on the little iron-bound box which was still lying where she had dropped it. He stooped down and opened it. A look of intense relief lightened his face. He picked it up and went out of the flat.

Left to itself the telephone rang again, insistently.

Chapter XVI

THE INQUEST

About ten minutes after Alleyn got back to his own flat that night, Nigel's call came through.

"Got you at last," he said.

"Did you ring up at Surbonadier's flat about twenty minutes after you left it?" asked Alleyn.

"Yes. How did you know?"

"I heard you."

"Well, why the deuce didn't you answer?"

"I was under the bed."

"What? This telephone's very bad."

"Never mind. What's the matter?"

"I've been to see Felix. He asked me to. You were right."

"Well, not over the telephone. Come to the Yard at nine to-morrow."

"All right," said Nigel. "Good night."

"Flights of angels sing thee to thy rest," said Alleyn wearily, and went to bed.

Next morning Nigel arrived at Scotland Yard with his copy and his messenger boy.

"This is becoming a habit," said Alleyn. He censored the story and the remains were dispatched to Fleet Street.

"Now," said Nigel, "listen!"

He told his story of Gardener's confession, and of the anonymous letter, which he produced. Alleyn listened attentively and examined the paper very carefully.

"I'm glad he decided to tell you this," he said. "Do you think he would repeat it and sign a statement to the same effect?"

"I think so. As far as I could gather, after he had got over the first shock of having killed Surbonadier, he began to think you'd suspect him of malice aforethought. Later on, after I'd heard Miss Vaughan ask him not to repeat whatever it was, he felt it was she who was in danger and that he must tell you everything he knew that would be likely to draw your suspicions away from her. He realises that what he has said definitely implicates Saint, and may implicate himself. He's not at all sure Saint did it. He's inclined to think it's suicide."

"So is our Mr. Saint—very much inclined," said Alleyn grimly. He pressed the bell on his desk.

"Ask Inspector Fox to come in," he said to the constable who answered it.

He examined the paper again in silence, until the inspector arrived.

"Glad tidings, Fox," said Alleyn. "Our little murderer

has come all over literary. He's writing letters. One begins to see a glim."

"Does one?" asked Nigel.

"But certainly. Fox, this letter arrived at Mr. Gardener's flat, by district messenger, at about eight-thirty last night. There's the envelope. The district messenger offices will have to be combed out. Have it tested for prints. You'll find Gardener and an 'unknown.' I've a pretty good idea who the unknown is."

"May I ask who?" Fox ventured eagerly.

"A man who, in all honesty, I think I may say we have never, in the course of our speculation, suspected of this crime; a man who, by his apparent eagerness to help the police, by his frequent suggestions, as well as by his singular charm of manner, has succeeded so far in escaping even our casual attention. And that man's name is——"

"You can search me, sir."

"Nigel Bathgate."

"You fatuous old bag of tripe!" shouted Nigel furiously. And then when he saw Fox's scandalised face: "I beg your pardon, inspector. Like Mr. Saint, I don't always appreciate your comedy. It is true, Inspector Fox," he added with quiet dignity, "that my fingerprints will be on that paper; but *not* all over it. Only at one edge, and then I remembered not to."

"You'll escape us this time, I'm afraid, sir," said Fox solemnly. He began to heave with subterranean chuckles. "Your face was a fair treat, Mr. Bathgate," he added.

"Well," said Alleyn, "having worked off my professional facetiousness, let's get down to it. In your list of properties offstage is there a typewriter?"

"There is. A Remington used in the first and last act."

"Where's it kept?"

"In the property-room, between whiles. I think they re-set the first act after the show, as a rule, so it would be on the stage when they all got down to the theatre, and in the property-room after the last act. We tested it for prints first, just in case it might be in the picture.

It showed Mr. Gardener's on the keys, and Props's prints at the sides, where he had carried it on."

"The fingerprints system's too well advertised nowadays for the poorest criminal to fall directly foul of it. Who used the typewriter in the last act? Oh, I remember—Gardener. Just let me get a copy of the letter and then give it to Bailey, will you, Fox? And get him to test the typewriter again. No, I'm not dotty. And now I must get things in order for the inquest. Thank the Lord it's a presentable coroner."

"Ah," agreed Fox heavily. "You may say that."

"How do you mean?" Nigel asked.

"Some of them," said Alleyn, "I positively believe, keep black caps in their hip pockets. Tiresome old creatures. However, this one is a sensible fellow, and we'll be through in no time."

"I'll get back to Fleet Street," said Nigel. "I'm meeting Felix and going to the inquest with him. His lawyer is going to be there."

"I expect there'll be a covey of 'em. My spies tell me St. Jacob has employed Phillip Phillips to watch the wheels go round. He's a brother of Phillips, K.C., who did St. Jacob so proud in the libel action. Very big game afoot."

"Well," said Nigel at the door, "we meet——"

"At Phillipi, in fact. *Au revoir*, Bathgate."

Nigel spent a couple of hours in his office, writing up cameo portraits of the leading characters in the case. His chief expressed himself as being not displeased with the stories, and Nigel, at twenty to eleven, went underground to Sloane Square, and thence to Gardener's flat. The lawyer, a young and preternaturally solemn one, was already there. They discussed a glass of sherry and Nigel attempted to enliven the occasion with a few *facetiæ*, which did not go down particularly well. The lawyer, whose unsuitably Congrevian name was Mr. Reckless, eyed him owlishly, and Gardener was too nervous and upset to be amused. They finished their sherry, and sought a taxi.

The inquest proved, on the whole, a disappointment

to the crowds of people who attended it. Very little information as regards police activity came out. Alleyn gave a concise account of the actual scene in the theatre, and was treated with marked respect by the coroner. Nigel watched his friend, and experienced something of the sensation that visited him as a small boy, when the chief god of Pop walked on to a dais and grasped the hand of Royalty. Alleyn described the revolver, and the cartridges—.455.

"Did you notice anything remarkable about either the weapon or the cartridges?" asked the coroner.

"They were the regulation .455, used in that type of Smith and Wesson. There were no fingerprints."

"A glove had been used?"

"Probably."

"What about the dummy cartridges?"

Alleyn described them, and said he had found traces of sand from the faulty cartridge in the prompt corner, and in both drawers.

"What do you deduce from that?"

"That the property master gave the dummies to the stage manager, who put them as usual in the top drawer."

"You suggest that someone afterwards moved them to the second drawer, replacing them with genuine cartridges?"

"Yes, sir."

"Is there anything else you noted as regards the cartridges?"

"I saw whitish stains on them."

"Have you any explanation for this?"

"I believe them to be caused by a certain cosmetic used as a hand make-up by actresses."

"Not by actors?"

"I imagine not. There was none in the actors' dressing-rooms?"

"You found bottles of this cosmetic in the actresses' dressing-rooms?"

"I did."

"Are the contents of these bottles all alike?"

"Not precisely."

132

" Could you distinguish from which, if any, of these bottles, the staines on the revolver had come?"

" An analysis shows that it came from the star dressing-room. A bottle of cosmetic had been spilt there, earlier in the evening."

" The star dressing-room is used—by whom?"

" By Miss Stephanie Vaughan and her dresser. Miss Vaughan received visits from other members of the company during the evening. I myself called on Miss Vaughan, before the first act. The cosmetic was not spilt then. I met, in this room, the deceased, who appeared to be under the influence of alcohol."

" Will you describe to the jury your investigations, immediately after the tragedy?"

Alleyn did so, at some length.

" You searched the stage. Did you find anything that threw any light on the matter?"

" I found a pair of gloves in a bag that had been used on the stage, and I found the dummy cartridges in a lower drawer of the desk."

" What did you remark about the gloves?"

" One had a white stain which, on analysis, proved to be similar to that on the cartridges."

This statement caused a stir among the onlookers. Alleyn's evidence went on for some time. He described his interviews with the performers, and said they had all since signed the notes taken at the time of their statements. This was news to Nigel, who wondered how they had reacted to the evidence of his activities. Alleyn said little about the subsequent investigations by the police, and was not pressed to do so by the coroner, who left him a very free hand.

Felix Gardener was called. He was very pale, but gave his evidence clearly. He admitted ownership of the revolver, said it was his brother's, and added that he gave the six cartridges to the property man, who converted them into dummies.

" Did you visit Miss Vaughan's dressing-room before the fatality?"

" Yes. I was there with Chief Detective-Inspector

Alleyn, who visited me with a friend, before the first act. I did not return after the first act."

"Did you notice a bottle of white cosmetic upset on the dressing-table?"

"No, sir."

"Mr. Gardener, will you describe the actual scene when you fired the revolver?"

Gardener did so. His voice shook over this, and he was very pale.

"Did you realise at once what had happened?"

"Not at once, I think," Gardener answered. "I was dazed with the report of the revolver. I think it flashed through my mind that one of the blanks, fired in the wings, had got into the chamber of the gun."

"You continued in the character of your part?"

"Yes," said Gardener in a low voice. "Quite automatically. Then I began to realise. But we went on."

"We?"

Gardener hesitated.

"Miss Vaughan was also on, in that scene."

A pair of grey suède gloves was produced, to the infinite satisfaction of the onlookers.

"Are those your property?"

"No." Gardener looked both surprised and relieved.

"Have you seen them before?"

"No. Not to my knowledge."

The anonymous letter was produced, and identified by Gardener, who described how it arrived and explained the reference to his "sore foot."

"Did you get any impression of the identity of the person who trod on your foot?"

Gardener hesitated, and glanced at Alleyn.

"I received a vague impression, but afterwards decided it was not definite enough to count for anything."

"Whom did this impression suggest?"

"Must I answer that?"

He looked again towards Alleyn.

"You told Chief Detective-Inspector Alleyn of this impression?"

"Yes. But I added that it really was not reliable."

"What name did you mention?"

"None. Inspector Alleyn asked if I noticed a particular scent. I thought I had done so."

"You meant a perfume of sorts?"

"Yes."

"With whom did you associate it?"

"With Mr. Jacob Saint."

Mr. Phillip Phillips was on his feet, in righteous indignation. The coroner dealt with him, and turned to Gardener.

"Thank you, Mr. Gardener."

Stephanie Vaughan appeared next. She was very composed and dignified, and gave here evidence lucidly. She confirmed everything that Alleyn had said as regards the stage-white and said that Surbonadier himself upset it after the others had gone. She believed it to be a case of suicide. The jury looked sympathetic and doubtful.

The rest of the cast followed in turn. Barclay Crammer gave a good all-round performance of a heart-broken gentleman of the old school. Janet Emerald achieved the feat known to leading ladies as "running through the gamut of the emotions." Asked to account for the striking discrepancies between her statement and those of Miss Max and the stage manager, she wept unfeignedly and said her heart was broken. The coroner stared at her coldly, and told her she was an unsatisfactory witness. Miss Deamer was youthfully sincere, and used a voice with an effective little broken gasp. Her evidence was supremely irrelevant. The stage manager and Miss Max were sensible and direct. Props looked and behaved so precisely like a murderer, that he left the box in a perfect gale of suspicion. Trixie Beadle struck the "I was an innocent girl" note, but was obviously frightened and was treated gently.

"You say you knew deceased well. You mean you were on terms of great intimacy?"

"I suppose you'd call it that," said poor Trixie.

Her father was sparse, respectful and rather pathetic. Howard Melville was earnest, sincere, and unhelpful.

Old Blair gave his evidence rather mulishly. He was asked to give the names of the people who went in at the stage door, and did so, including those of Inspector Alleyn, Mr. Bathgate, and Mr. Jacob Saint. Had he noticed anybody wearing these gloves come in at the stage door?

"Yes," said old Blair, in a bored voice.

"Who was this person?"

"Mr. Saint."

"Mr. Jacob Saint? (If there is a repetition of this noise, I shall have the court cleared.) Are you certain of this?"

"Yes," said old Blair and withdrew.

Mr. Jacob Saint stated that he was the proprietor of the theatre, that deceased was his nephew, and that he had seen him before the show. He indentified the gloves as his, and said he had left them behind the scenes. He did not know where. He had visited Miss Emerald's room, but did not think he was wearing them then. Probably he had put them down somewhere on the stage. To Nigel's surprise no mention was made of the tension between Saint and Surbonadier. Mincing, the footman, was not called. Mr. Saint had not returned to the stage until after the tragedy.

The coroner summed up at some length. He touched on the possibility of suicide, and rather belittled it. He directed the jury discreetly towards the verdict which, after an absence of twenty minutes, they ultimately returned— a verdict of murder against some person or persons unknown. As he left the court Nigel found himself walking behind Alleyn, and immediately in front of Janet Emerald and Saint. He was about to join the inspector when Miss Emerald pushed past him, and seized Alleyn by the arm.

"Inspector Alleyn," she said.

Alleyn stopped and looked at her.

"*You* were behind that." She spoke quietly enough, but with a kind of suppressed violence. "*You* told that man to treat me as he did. Why was I singled out to be insulted and suspected? Why was Felix Gardener let off so lightly? Why isn't he arrested? He shot Arthur. It's infamous." Her voice rose hysterically. Several people who had passed them stopped and looked back.

"Janet," said Saint hurriedly, "are you mad? Come away."

She turned and stared at him, burst into a passion of the most hair-raising sobs, and allowed herself to be led off.

Alleyn looked after her thoughtfully.

"Not mad, Mr. Saint," he murmured. "No. I don't think the Emerald is mad. Shall we say venomous to the point of foolhardiness?"

He followed them out into the street, without noticing Nigel.

Chapter XVII

SLOANE STREET TO THE YARD

Nigel spent the afternoon in writing up his report of the inquest. He was greatly intrigued by the vast amount of information that had *not* come out. The coroner had skated nimbly over the Jacob Saint libel action, had made no comment at all on Surbonadier's state of intoxication, and had walked like Aga in and out of Stephanie Vaughan's dressing-room. The jury, an unusually docile one, had apparently felt no urge to ask independent questions. Their foreman, like the Elephant's Child, had the air of saying "this is too butch for be." Nigel imagined that, in their brief retirement, they had discussed the possibility of suicide, decided it wouldn't wash, and agreed that the whole thing was too complex for any decision but the usual one, which they had given. He had sensed Alleyn's extreme satisfaction; and now, once more, revised his own view of the case.

He found that he had made up his mind that Saint was responsible for the murder. Yet Saint's was the best of all the alibis. He had been alone in the audience, but Blair had sworn positively that he had not seen the proprietor of the Unicorn return to the stage between the acts. Saint had been in a box, and it was just possible that he could have slipped out during the black-out. At this point Nigel got his brain-wave. Suppose Jacob Saint had left his box under cover of the black-out and had gone through the door in the proscenium, on to the stage. This door had been locked when Stavely and Nigel went through, but Saint might easily have got hold of a key. There he would be, before the lights went out, in his box facing the audience, as large as life. Then complete darkness. Saint had left the box, slipped through the door, which he had perhaps previously unlocked, gone straight to the desk, colliding with Gardener on the way, pulled out the drawers and replaced the dummies with the cartridges. When the lights went up again—there was Mr. Saint sitting in his box at the Unicorn. Nigel was thrilled with himself and rang up Scotland Yard. Alleyn was out, but had made an appointment for four o'clock. Nigel said he would be there at 4.30.

He felt fidgety and unable to settle down to anything. He was big with his theory. Presently he thought of Felix Gardener, and decided to walk round to Sloane Street and talk it over with him. He didn't ring up. If Felix was out he would walk on down to Knightsbridge and take a bus to the Yard. He wanted exercise.

Sloane Square, that full stop between Eatonia and Chelsea, had a look of sunny friendliness. Nigel bought a carnation for his coat, sent a silly telegram to his Angela, and walked lightly onwards. Sloane Street, with its air of quality and hint of boredom, was busier than usual. Nigel felt a sudden inclination to run, to whistle, to twirl his stick round. He glanced jauntily at a shabby-genteel man, who stood looking into the furniture shop next the flat. Gardener's windows on the first floor were open. He spoke blithely to the commissionaire, refused the lift, and ran two steps at a time up the thickly-carpeted stairs to Gardener's door.

It was open and Nigel, without ringing, went into the

little entrance hall that opened into the studio sitting-room. He was about to call out, cheerfully, and had actually drawn in his breath to do so, when he was brought up short by a woman's voice coming from the studio room.

"If I did it," it cried urgently, "it was for you—for you, Felix. He was your worst enemy."

Nigel heard Gardener say slowly: "I can't believe it. I can't believe it."

The woman began to laugh.

"All for nothing!" she said, between paroxysms of choking. "Never mind—I don't regret it. Do you hear that? But I don't think you were worth it."

Scarcely aware of what he did, and consious only of cataclysmic panic, Nigel banged the front door, and heard himself shout:

"Hullo, Felix, are you at home?"

Dead silence and then a sound of footsteps, and the studio door was thrown open.

"Oh—it's you, Nigel," said Felix Gardener.

Nigel didn't look at him, but beyond, into the studio, where he saw Stephanie Vaughan, very attractive, in an arm-chair by the window. She held a handkerchief to her lips.

"Why, it's Nigel Bathgate," she cried, with exactly the same inflexion as the one she used when she said: "Hullo, all you people," in her first entrance in the play.

"You've—you've met before," said Gardener.

Nigel managed to say something, even to take the hand she held out cordially towards him.

"I only came in for a second," he told Gardener.

"I'm sure you didn't," said Miss Vaughan gaily. "You've come to have a boy friend chat—the sort that consists of drinks, cigarettes, long silences and a few risqué stories. I'm off, anyway, so you needn't bother about me."

She rose to her feet in one lithe movement. She looked Nigel full in the face, and gave him the three-cornered smile.

"Make Felix bring you to see me," she commanded. "I rather like you, Nigel Bathgate. Felix—you hear? You're to bring him to see me."

"Is this your purse?" asked Gardener. Nigel saw him put it on a table near her, and knew he didn't want to touch her hand. He opened the door to her and she floated out, still talking. Gardener followed her, shut the door, and Nigel heard her voice, very low, outside. In another second the outer door slammed, and Gardener came back into the room.

"It was decent of you to come, Nigel," he said. "I'm all in."

He looked it. He sat down in front of the fire and held his hands to it. Nigel saw he was shaking:

"I think you ought to see a doctor, Felix," he ventured.

"No, no. It's only the after-effects of shock, I imagine. I'll be all right. Think I'll turn in presently and try for a little sleep. I haven't been able to sleep much."

"Jolly sound idea. Why don't you carry it out now? I'll give you some aspirin and a stiff whisky, and leave you in peace."

"Oh. in a minute. Any news?"

They had both managed to avoid speaking of Miss Vaughan. Nigel's theory about Saint came into his mind. He smiled rather wryly to himself at the remembrance of his so recent enthusiasm. Did Gardener wonder if he had overheard anything? Nigel believed that idea had not entered his friend's head. As Felix himself said, he was suffering from shock. Nigel forced himself to speak at random. It was hard to find anything to talk about. He who, hitherto, had barely impinged upon the edge of the theatrical world now found himself drawn into it. He felt, suddenly, as though he were surrounded by these people, as though, against his will, he was obliged to witness a play they had staged and as though he had been compelled to leave his seat in the auditorium and mingle confusedly with the action of the piece. The two men must have been silent for some time, for Nigel was startled to hear Gardener say suddenly:

"She gave her evidence well, didn't she?"

"Who?"

"Stephanie."

"Very well."

Some inflexion in Nigel's voice arrested Gardener's attention. He looked at his friend with a kind of agony in his eyes.

"Nigel—you remember what I said. Neither of us is guilty. I gave you my word and you said you believed me."

"I know I did," said Nigel miserably.

"Are you beginning—to wonder?"

"Are you *sure* you're right, Felix? She—— Oh, Lord!"

Gardener laughed.

"You *are* beginning to wonder. My God, if you only knew what a heroine she is!"

"Can't you come clean, Felix?"

"I can't—I can't. Not about Stephanie. Oh, well, I suppose I can't blame you. It looks pretty damning, for both of us. What does Alleyn say about the suicide theory?"

"He tells me very little," said Nigel.

"The verdict of the inquest was wrong," Gardener said urgently. "It was suicide. I'll see Alleyn myself and try and make him——" He broke off short. "He must be made to accept that it was suicide."

"I must go. Do try and get some sleep, Felix."

"Sleep! 'Sleep that knits up the ravelled sleeve of care.' Ugh! There goes the actor! Good-bye, Nigel."

"I'll let myself out. Good-bye."

Nigel walked sombrely downstairs and out again into Sloane Street.

He realised now that he had a terrible decision to make. Was he to tell Alleyn of the conversation he had overheard? A woman! He shied off the logical consequence of his statement, and then, despising himself, came back to it again. If he held his tongue what would happen? Would Felix, who loved her, let Saint be accused of the murder? He thought of Alleyn's attitude towards his scruples, and suddenly realised that it was his own peace of mind that he was trying to salvage. He was in Knightsbridge, and walking down to Hyde Park Corner, when he made his decision. He had no right to withhold his knowledge. He would tell Alleyn. With a heavy heart he stopped a taxi.

"Scotland Yard," he said.

It was not yet four o'clock when he got there, but the chief inspector was in and could see him. He went up at once.

"Hullo, Bathgate," Alleyn said. "What's the matter with you? Found the murderer again?"

"Please don't rag me," Nigel begged him. "It's not a theory I've come to give you. It's a statement."

"Sit down. Now then, what is it?"

"I suppose you won't understand how awful this feels, Alleyn. To you, it's all got to be completely impersonal. I can't feel like that. It's been rather an effort to come to you with this information. That sounds theatrical, I know, but you see—it's a woman."

"What do you mean?" said Alleyn harshly. "What's this information? You say you've got a statement to make—well, make it. I beg your pardon, Bathgate—I'm unbearable these days, aren't I?"

Nigel gulped.

"I've overheard a confession," he said.

Alleyn waited a second, and then took up a pencil.

"When?"

"This afternoon about an hour ago."

"Where?"

"At Felix's flat."

"All right. Go ahead."

"It's soon told. I went up into his little lobby, without knocking and I heard voices in the 'studio' as he calls it. A woman said : 'If I did, it was for you, Felix. He was your worst enemy.' Felix said : 'I can't believe it. I can't believe it,' and she began to laugh, horribly, and said : 'It was all for nothing. Never mind, I don't regret it.' Do you hear that? But I don't think you were worth it.' Then I shut the front door noisily and called out. Felix came and let me in. She was there."

" It was——?"

" Stephanie Vaughan."

" Impossible," said Alleyn fiercely.

" You don't think I could make a mistake over a thing like that, do you? I tell you I'll never forget their voices for as long as I live."

Alleyn was silent for so long that Nigel stared at him in some discomfort. He looked as though he had made a shutter of his face. At last he said :

" After all, Bathgate, this is not conclusive. 'If I did, it was for you. He was your worst enemy.' Suppose she had told Gardener that she had used some threat to Surbonadier, to choke him off, and that she believed she had driven him to suicide? Suppose they were not speaking of Surbonadier?"

" If you had seen Felix you wouldn't suggest that."

" Why—what do you mean?"

" He's a broken man," said Nigel simply.

" A broken man! A broken man! You're getting as stagy as any of them. Barclay Crammer was a 'broken man ' in the witness-box this morning, silly old ass."

Nigel got up.

" Well, that's all," he said. " If you don't think it's conclusive, I'm damn' thankful."

Alleyn leant over the desk and looked at him as though he were a museum piece.

" If Diogenes had rolled up against you," he observed, " he'd have got out of this barrel, filled it with booze and made whoopee."

" I suppose you mean to be nice," said Nigel in a relieved voice.

" I suppose I do. What happened afterwards?"

" We made perfectly dreadful conversation. I must say she gave a marvellous performance."

" I believe you."

" She asked me to go and see her." Nigel shuddered.

" You're not to go."

" Am I likely to?"

" Listen to me. You're to pay no more visits to these people. Understand?"

"Yes—but what's biting you?"

"Unless I'm with you. Write your little articles, and mind your little business."

"This is what I get for doing the beastliest job of my life."

"My dear Bathgate, I do honestly appreciate your difficulty and am genuinely grateful," said Inspector Alleyn, with one of his rather charming turns of formality. "But I do ask you to behave as I suggest. I can reward you with a very choice bit of copy."

"What's that?"

"You may inform your public that Mr. Jacob Saint has been arrested, but that the nature of the charge is not known."

Chapter XVIII

ARREST

"As a matter of hard fact," Alleyn continued, when he had noted, with satisfaction, Nigel's dropped jaw, "Mr. Saint is still at large. I am just off now to do my stuff. Care to come?"

"You bet I would. May I just ring up the office? I'll catch the stop press for the last edition."

"Very well. Say no more than what I've told you. You'd better warn them to hold it back for another twenty minutes. If he's not arrested, you can ring up. Aren't I good to you?"

"Very," said Nigel fervently. He rang up and was well received. "That's that," he said.

"Well, we must hustle along as soon as I get the word from my myrmidon. Don't let me forget my handcuffs. Dear me, I'm quite excited!"

"Five minutes ago," observed Nigel, "you looked as though I'd punched you between the eyes. What's come over you?"

" I've taken thought, or rose leaves, or something, and am ' no longer a Golden Ass '."

" Are you arresting Saint for the murder?"

" *Wouldn't* you like to know?"

A single knock on the door heralded the entrance of Inspector Fox.

" Our man's just rung up," he said. " The gentleman is in the office of the Unicorn. 'Evening, Mr. Bathgate."

" Away we go then," cried Alleyn.

" Handcuffs," said Nigel.

" What would I do without you! Handcuffs, Fox?"

" Have got. You'd better put your top coat on, Chief. It's a cold evening."

" Here's the warrant," murmured Alleyn. He struggled into his overcoat and pulled on his felt hat at a jaunty angle.

" Am I tidy?" he asked. " It looks so bad not to be tidy for an arrest."

Nigel thought dispassionately, that he looked remarkably handsome, and wondered if the chief inspector had " It." " I must ask Angela," thought Nigel.

Alleyn led the way into the passage. Inspector Fox took the opportunity to say, in a hoarse whisper :

" He's very worried over this case, Mr. Bathgate. You always know. All this funny business." He had the air of a Nannie, discussing her charge.

A policeman and two plain clothes men awaited them. " Unicorn Theatre," said Alleyn.

" There's a couple of those blasted Pressmen outside," said Fox as they started. " Begging your pardon, Mr. Bathgate."

" Oh," said Alleyn, " we'll go in at the little street behind the theatre. It connects with one of the exits. We can go through the stalls. into the office. Bathgate, you can walk round to the front and swap a bit of agony column with your brother-pests, and then come down the stage door alley-way, all casual. Show this card to the officer on duty there, and he'll let you in. You'll get there as soon as we do. Spin them a yarn."

" Watch me!" said Nigel enthusiastically.

Alleyn gave Fox an account of Nigel's experience in the Sloane Street flat. Fox stared at Nigel as though he was an adventurous child.

The car threaded its way through a maze of narrow streets. Presently Fox tapped on the window, and they stopped.

"This is the back of the Unicorn," said Alleyn. "Out you get, Bathgate. Up there, and round to the left, will bring you out in front. I'll give you a start."

Nigel was conscious that his heart beat thickly as he ran up the side street. He dropped into a walk as he turned towards the impressive modern front of the theatre, with its bas-relief, in black glass and steel, of a star-spotted unicorn. There, sure enough, were two brother-journalist both of whom he knew slightly.

"Nosing round?" asked Nigel cheerfully.

"And you?" answered one politely.

"I've got a date with the comedienne. If you watch this alley-way, you may see something to your advantage."

"What are you up to?" they asked him suspiciously. "You with your pals in the force."

"Watch me, and see."

He walked airily down the stage door alley-way, till he came to a side door into the front of the house. A uniformed constable was on duty here. He assumed a patiently reproachful air as Nigel drew near him, but when he read Alleyn's card, he grinned and opened the door.

"Straight up those stairs," he said.

Nigel cocked a snook at his friends and walked in.

The stairs, which were heavily carpeted, ran up to the dress circle foyer. Here Nigel found Alleyn, Fox, and the two plain clothes detectives, talking to a fifth man whom he had not seen before.

"He came along about a quarter of an hour ago," this man said quietly. "I was up here, but I told the P.C. downstairs to let him in. He looked sideways at me, and asked me when the police were going to clear out and let him have the run of his own property. He said there were letters waiting for him which he must attend to.

I made difficulties and held him here. My man downstairs was instructed to ring the Yard as soon as Saint walked into the trap. He's just gone along now, sir, into the office at the end of that passage."

"Well done," said Alleyn. "Come along."

"You got a gun, sir?" asked Fox.

"No. I knew you'd have one, you old blood-thirster. Bathgate, you follow last, will you?"

They walked in silence down the long passage. Nigel was acutely aware of the odour of officialdom. Suddenly, these men whom he knew and liked had become simply policeman. "They are walking in step, I do believe," thought Nigel.

They stopped outside a steel-framed door. He could hear somebody moving about on the other side.

Alleyn knocked once, turned the handle, and walked in. The others followed, Fox with his hand in his jacket pocket.

Between their shoulders Nigel saw Jacob Saint. He had his bowler hat on, and a cigar in his mouth. He seemed to have swung round from a heap of papers on an opened desk.

"What's this?" he said.

The other officers moved apart. Alleyn walked up to him.

"Mr. Saint," he said quietly, "I have a warrant for your arrest——"

Saint made some sort of incoherent sound. Alleyn paused.

"You're mad," said Saint thickly. "I didn't do it. I wasn't there. I was in front."

"Before you go any further, you had better hear the charge."

Saint dropped into the swivel chair. He looked quickly from one man to another. His hand fumbled at the side of the desk.

"You're covered, Mr. Saint," Fox remarked suddenly. With something like a sneer, the proprietor of the Unicorn let his hands drop on to the arms of his chair.

"What's the charge?" he asked.

"You are charged with being concerned with traffic in illicit drugs. Read it out, please. Fox. I get the language wrong."

Thus urged, Inspector Fox broke instantly into a monotonous sing-song to which Saint listened closely, feasting unattractively the while on his little finger-nail.

"It's infamous," he said, when Fox had stopped as abruptly as he began. "It's infamous. You—Alleyn. You'll make a laughing-stock of yourself over this. You'll lose your job."

"And that'll learn me," said Alleyn. "Come along, Mr. Saint."

Saint took his hand from his lips and let it fall to the lapel of his coat. He rose ponderously, and half turned aside.

The next second Alleyn had him by the wrist. The thick fingers held a piece of paper.

"Please, Mr. Saint," said Alleyn. "We can't have you eating paper, you know."

The next second they were struggling bitterly. Saint seemed to have gone mad. In a moment the chair was overturned. The two men had crashed across the desk. An inkpot fell to the floor, splashing Saint's light check trousers. The other men had got hold of him. Alleyn still held his wrist. It was now strained across his back, making the rolls of fat and muscle on his arm and shoulder bulge. He stopped struggling abruptly.

"Pick up that chair," Alleyn ordered sharply. Nigel, who had hovered impotently on the outskirts of the battle, set the heavy swivel chair on its feet.

"Let him down gently. You'll be all right, Mr. Saint. Open those windows, one of you."

Saint lay back in the chair. His face was purple and his breathing terribly distressed. Alleyn took off his tie, and unfastened his collar. The pulse in his neck throbbed laboriously. Alley loosened his clothes and stood looking at him. Then he turned to the desk telephone and dialled a number.

"Yard? Chief Inspector Alleyn. Get the divisional surgeon to come round to the Unicorn Theatre at once.

Heart attack, tell him. Got that? Upstairs. The constable at the door will show him. At once. Thank you." He put the receiver down.

"You'd better go outside, I think," said Alleyn. "He wants to be quiet. Fox, will you wait here?"

The three detectives filed out quietly. Fox stood still. Nigel walked over to the darkest corner and sat down, hoping to remain unnoticed.

"Heart attack?" asked Fox quietly.

"Evidently. He'll do though, I fancy." They looked in silence at the empurpled face. Alleyn switched on an electric fan and moved it across the desk. Saint's thin hair was blown sideways. He opened his eyes. They were terribly bloodshot.

"Don't try to talk," said Alleyn. "A doctor will be here in a moment."

He pulled forward another chair, put Saint's feet on it, and then moved him a little, until he was almost lying flat. He did all this very quickly and efficiently, lifting the huge bulk without apparent effort. Then he moved across to the window. Nigel saw that he held the piece of paper. Alleyn leant out of the window, looked at it, and then put it in his pocket.

The room was very silent: Saint was breathing more easily. Presently he gave a deep sigh and closed his eyes again. Fox walked over to Alleyn, who spoke to him in a low voice. The electric fan made a high, thrumming noise and blandly turned from side to side. Saint's hair blew out in fine strands, fell, and blew out again, regularly. Nigel stared at Saint's heavy face, and wondered if it was the face of a murderer.

Before long they heard voices in the passage outside. The door opened and the divisional surgeon came in. He walked over to Saint and bent down to make an examination. He took the pulse, holding up the fat, white wrist and looking placidly at his watch. Then he injected something. Saint's lips parted and came together again clumsily.

"Better," he whispered breathlessly.

"I think so," said the doctor. "We'll keep you quiet

149

a little longer and then take you away, where you'll be more comfortable."

He looked at Alleyn and the others.

"We'll leave him for a moment, I think," he said. They went out of the room. Nigel followed, leaving Fox, who shut the door. They walked along the passage a little way.

"Yes, it's his heart," said the doctor. "It's pretty nasty. He's a sick man. Who his doctor."

"Sir Everard Sim," said Alleyn.

"Oh, yes. Well, he'd better see him. Is he under arrest?"

"He is."

"H'm. Nuisance. I'll get an ambulance and wait for him. Leave me a couple of men. I'll ring up Sir Everard. Saint's pretty dickey, but he'll pull round."

"Right," said Alleyn. "You'll fix up here then, will you? I'll leave Fox to see to it."

"Oh," said the doctor, "while I think of it. There's a message for you at the Yard. They asked me to tell you. Someone called Albert Hickson is very anxious to see you. It's about this case. He wouldn't talk to anyone else."

"Albert Hickson," Nigel exclaimed. "Why, that's Props!"

"Hullo," said Alleyn, "you've come to life, have you? You've no business here at all. I must get back to the Yard."

Nigel retreated, but he managed to slip innocently back into the car with Alleyn, who raised no objection. The chief inspector was rather silent. As they drew near Scotland Yard he turned to Nigel.

"Bathgate," he said, "is your news of the arrest out by now?"

"Yes," Nigel assured him. "I didn't ring up to stop it— it will be all over London already. Wonderful, isn't it?" he added modestly.

"All over London already. Yes. That'll be it," murmured Alleyn.

Nigel followed him, dog-like, into the Yard. The man who had seen Props was produced.

"Was he carrying a newspaper?"

"Yes, sir."

"Notice which one?"

The constable had noticed and was eager to say so. Props had carried Nigel's paper.

"You're rather wasted at this job," said Alleyn curtly. "You use your eyes."

The constable flushed with pleasure, and produced a sheet of paper.

"He left this message, sir, and said that he'd call again."

"Thank you."

Nigel, still hopeful, followed Alleyn to his room. At the door Alleyn paused politely.

"May I come in?" he asked. "Or do you wish to be alone?"

Nigel assumed the frank and manly deportment of an eager young American in a crook film. He gazed raptly at Alleyn, wagged his head sideways, and said with emotion:

"Gee, Chief, you're—you're a regular guy."

"Aw, hell, buddy," snarled Alleyn. "C'm on in."

Once in his room, he took out a file, opened it, and laid beside it the paper he had taken from Saint, and the one Props had left at the Yard.

"What's that?" asked Nigel.

"With your passion for the word I think you would call it a dossier. It's the file of the Unicorn murder."

"And you're going to add those fresh documents?" Nigel strolled up to the desk.

"Can you read from there?" asked Alleyn anxiously "Or shall I put them closer?"

Nigel was silent.

"The Saint exhibit is a second letter from Mortlake that lands St. Jacob with a crash at the botom of his ladder. The note from Props——" Alleyn paused.

"Well?"

"Oh, there you are."

Nigel read the following message, written in rather babyish characters:

I know who done it and you got the wrong man. J. Saint never done it you did not ought to of arrested an innocent man yrs respectfully A. Hickson.

"What's it mean?" asked Nigel

"It means Props will shortly pay a call on the murderer," said Alleyn.

Chapter XIX

NIGEL WARNED OFF

"Now, don't start badgering me with questions," begged Alleyn. "If you must stay, stay quiet. I've got work to do." He pressed his bell, hung up his hat, and lit a cigarette. Then he took off the receiver of his telephone.

"Give me Inspector Boys. Hullo, is that you, Boys? Who's shadowing that fellow Hickson? Oh, Thompson, is it? When is he relieved? That's in about a quarter of an hour. Has he rung up? He has! Where is he? I see. Thank you very much."

To the constable who answered the bell he said: "Ask the man who saw Hickson to come and speak to me."

The man in question appeared in remarkably short time. He stood to attention like a private soldier. Nigel was reminded of Props.

"What's you name?" Alleyn asked.

"Naseby, sir."

"Well, Naseby, I've got a job for you. You know Thompson?"

"Yes, sir."

"He's shadowing Hickson—the man you saw this afternoon. At the moment they are both in an eating-house at the corner of Westbourne Street and the Pimlico Road. Go there in a taxi. Wait till Hickson comes out, and then run across him casually in the street. Recognise him and say you're going off duty. Get into conversation, if you can, but don't let him suspect you. Tell him you gave me his note and you don't think it's much use his coming back here. Say you overheard me remark to Mr. Bathgate here that I thought he was a bit touched and that we've got the right man. Say I told you to tell him I couldn't see him if he came back. I want him to think I'm quite uninterested in him and his information. He's only just gone in there—you may be in time to sit down by him and stand him a drink. Say, in your opinion, Saint will hang. Don't try and pump him—treat the matter as settled. Then let him go. The detective who relieves Thompson must carry on, and tell him from me if he loses his man I'll murder him. He's not to come away until he's certain Hickson is bedded down for the night. Then he can ring up, and we'll relieve him. He is to note down most particularly the number of every house Props—I mean Hickson—goes to. The more information he can get the better I'll be pleased. Now, do you understand?"

"Yes, sir. I'll just go over it if I may, sir."

"Right."

Naseby repeated his instructions, quickly and accurately.

"That's it," said Alleyn. "Now, away you go. Come here when you return. He's a smart fellow, that," he added when Naseby had gone.

He next asked for a report from the district messenger offices that had been combed through that afternoon.

The anonymous letter to Gardener was traced to an office in Piccadilly. They had been particularly busy when the gentleman called and hadn't much noticed him. He had worn an overcoat, a muffler, a soft hat, and gloves. He had put the letter on the counter and said: "See that's delivered at once. The boy can keep the change. I'm in a hurry." and had gone out. Height? Medium. Voice? couldn't really say. Clean-shaven? They thought so. Figure? Perhaps on the stout side. "Ugh?" said Alleyn. "Our old pal, the man in the street. Might be anybody."

He sent for Detective-Sergeant Bailey, who came in looking puzzled.

"About that typewriter," he said at once. "It's a rum

thing. There's no doubt about it; the anonymous letter was written on the machine in the theatre. We tested that machine on the night of the affair, and found only Mr. Gardener's and Prop's prints. Mr. Gardener used it in the play, so that was all right. Well, according to your instructions, sir, we've tested it again, and it's got no prints on the keyboard at all now, except on the letter Q, which still has Mr. Gardener's. I couldn't make it out at all, at first, but I reckon I've got an idea now."

"Yes? What is it, Bailey?"

"Well, sir—after we'd tested the machine it was put into the property-room. All the actors, as you know, were in the wardrobe-room. But Jacob Saint wasn't. He came in afterwards. Now, suppose he went into the property-room and rattled that off? The doors were shut. We wouldn't hear him on the stage, and it would only take a second or two. The paper was in the machine. He could put it in his pocket—you'd already searched him—and go off comfortably. The letter Q is out at the side, and he'd miss it when he wiped his prints off the keys."

"Where is the property-room?" asked Nigel.

"All down that passage to the stage door. It's a dock really. Big double doors open on to the stage, and beyond old Blair's perch, there are other doors opening into the yard. See what I mean, sir? When Saint goes off with Miss Emerald he passes our man at the stage door, goes out into the yard, and slips into the dock by the pilot door that's cut in the big ones. The double doors on to the stage are shut. He turns on one light, types his letter, wipes over the keys, and slips out. And that dame knows what he's doing and keeps a look out."

"Still after the Emerald, I see," said Alleyn.

Nigel remembered his theory about Saint and the proscenium door. He advanced it modestly and was listened to by Detective Bailey with a kind of grudging respect peculiar to that official.

"Well," said Alleyn, "it's possible, Bailey. But any of the others could have done the typewriter business—or, at any rate, some of them could. Simpson could, for instance. Think a moment. Who was nearest to the stage door and most able to slip out unnoticed?"

Bailey stared at him.

"Gosh!" he said at last.

"*You mean—old Blair*?" Nigel said slowly.

"Who was asleep," added Alleyn placidly. The other two gaped at him.

"Well," said Alleyn, "nothing's conclusive, but everything is healthier. It all begins to come together very nicely."

"Glad you're pleased, sir," said Bailey with unexpected sarcasm.

"What about prints on the letter?"

"Only Mr. Gardener and Mr. Bathgate."

"And the paper from Surbonadier's flat? The one with the forged signature?"

"Plenty of Mr. Surbonadier's, sir, and something else that's very distinct and old. I'm having an enlarged photograph taken and can't give an opinion till I've got it. It may turn out to be the deceased, too."

"Let me know at once if it is, Bailey. I'd like to see the photograph."

"Very good, sir."

Bailey was at the door when Alleyn stopped him.

"By the way, Bailey," he said, "I suppose you've heard that we couldn't get any forrader with the cartridges. Inspector Fox tells me every gunsmith's and sports shop in the country has been probed."

"That's right, sir. Very unsatisfactory," said Bailey, and withdrew.

"Alleyn," said Nigel, after a pause, "can't you *force* Props to say whom he saw moving round in the dark?"

"I could try, but he can so easily say he doesn't know who it was. His words were: 'If I thought I saw a bloke, or it might have been a woman, moving round in the dark . . .' Not very conclusive."

"But surely he now thinks you've got the wrong man, and will tell you who it was, to save Saint."

"He's very anxious," said Alleyn, "to save—the murderer."

"Who is probably Saint," said Nigel. "I see. But what about Stephanie Vaughan? Alleyn, if you'd heard her as I did—— Oh, by God, I believe she did it! I believe she did."

"Look here, Bathgate. Could you take a day off to-morrow and go into the country on a job for me?"

"Not possible," said the astonished Nigel. "What sort of job? I've got my own job, you might remember."

"I want you to go to High Wycombe and see if you can trace a man called Septimus Carewe."

"You want to get rid of me," said Nigel indignantly. "Septimus Carewe, my foot!" he added with conviction.

"I mean it."

"What on earth for!"

"I'm uneasy about you."

"Bosh!"

"Have it you own way."

"What are *you* doing to-morrow, may I ask?"

"I," said Alleyn, "am putting on a show at the Unicorn."

"What the devil do you mean?"

"The company is under notice to report at various police stations every day. They have all been asked to report at the Unicorn at eleven to-morrow. I intend to hold a reconstruction of the murder."

"As you did in the Frantock case?"

"The conditions are very different. In this instance I am simply using the characters to prove my theory. In the Arthur Wilde case I forced his confession. This, unless these unspeakable mummers insist on dramatising themselves, will be less theatrical."

"I shall be there, however."

"I don't want you there."

"Why ever not?"

"It's a very unpleasant business. I loathe homicide cases and the result of this investigation will be perfectly beastly."

"If I could stand the Frantock case, when my own cousin was murdered, I can stand this."

"You'd much better keep away."

"I do think you're bloody," said Nigel fretfully.

Fox came in.

"Hullo," said Alleyn. "Everything fixed up?"

"Yes. Saint's tucked up in bed and the specialist's been sent for."

"I've just been telling Mr. Bathgate," said Alleyn, "that I don't want him at the theatre to-morrow, and he's got the huff in consequence."

"Inspector Alleyn's quite right, sir," said Fox. "You'd better keep clear of this business. After what you overheard this morning."

"Do you suppose Miss Vaughan is going to ram an arsenic chocolate down my maw?"

The two detectives exchanged a look.

"Oh, well, I'm off," said Nigel angrily.

"Good evening," said Alleyn cheerfully.

Nigel allowed himself the doubtful luxury of slamming the door.

Once out in the street he began to feel rather foolish, and angrier then ever with Chief Detective-Inspector Alleyn for causing this uncomfortable sensation. It was now seven o'clock and Nigel was hungry. He walked rapidly to Regent Street and went into the downstairs restaurant at the Hungaria, where he had a morose and extravagant dinner. He ordered himself brandy, and a cigar which he did not want and did not enjoy. When these were exhausted Nigel called for his bill, tipped his waiter, and marched out of the restaurant.

"Damn it," he said to Lower Regent Street. "I'm going there to-morrow whether he likes it or not."

He took a taxi to his flat in Chester Terrace.

Chief Detective-Inspector Alleyn also dined alone, at a restaurant near the Yard. He returned to his room soon after eight, opened the file of the Unicorn case and went over it very carefully with Inspector Fox. They were two hours at this business. Naseby came in and reported. He had seen Props and had brought off his conversation nicely. Props had seemed very much upset and when last seen was walking in the direction of the King's Road. Naseby had seen him go into a telephone-box and had then left him to Detective Thompson, who preferred to carry on without being relieved.

Alleyn and Fox returned to the file. Bit by bit they strung together the events of the last three days, and Alleyn talked and Fox listened. At one stage he cast himself back in his chair and stared for fully ten seconds at his superior.

" Do you agree?" asked Alleyn.

" Oh, yes," said Fox heavily, " I agree."

He thought for a moment and then he said:

" I've been thinking that in difficult homicide cases you either get no motive or too many motives. In this instance there are too many. Jacob Saint had been blackmailed by the deceased; Stephanie Vaughan was pestered and threatened. Trixie Beadle was probably ruined by him; Props was what lawyers called ' deeply wronged.' So was the girl's father. That Emerald woman gets Saint's money by it. Well, I don't mind owning I've had my eye on all of 'em in turn. There you are."

" I know," said Alleyn, " I've been though the same process myself. Now look here, Fox. It seems to me there are one or two key pieces in this puzzle. One is the, to me, inexplicable fact that Surbonadier kept that sheet of paper with the experimental signatures: Edward Wakeford, Edward Wakeford, Edward Wakeford. I say inexplicable, in the light of any theory that has been advanced. Another is the evidence of the prints on the typewriter. A third is the behaviour of Stephanie Vaughan last night in Surbonadier's flat. Why did she pretend one of her letters was missing and get me hunting for it? I may tell you I left a folded piece of plain paper in the iron-bound box. While I was out of the room she took that paper. Why? Because she thought it was the document she was after."

" The Mortlake letter or the signatures?"

" Not the Mortlake letter. Why should she risk all that to save Saint?"

" The signatures then?"

" I think so. Now put that together with the fragment of conversation Mr. Bathgate overheard this morning, and what do you get?"

" The *fragment* of conversation," said Fox slowly.

" Exactly."

" I believe you're right, sir. But have you got enough to put before a jury?"

" I've got a man down at Cambridge now, ferreting about in past history. If he fails I'm still going for it. The reconstruction to-morrow morning will help."

" But he won't be there—Saint, I mean."

" *You* are going to climb Jacob's ladder for me to-morrow, my Foxkin."

The telephone rang. Alleyn answered it.

" Hullo. Yes. Where? But what about our men at the doors? Simon's Alley. I see. Well, get back to it and if he comes out detain him. I'll be there. No, don't go in alone. How long have you left the place? I see. Get back there quickly."

Alleyn clapped the receiver down.

" Fox," he said, " we're going to the Unicorn."

" Now?"

" Yes, and damn' quick. I'll tell you on the way."

Chapter XX

EXIT PROPS

" After Naseby left the King's Road," said Alleyn, when they were in the car, " Thompson watched Props in the telephone-box. He put two calls through. As soon as he had gone Thompson went in and asked for the numbers. The operator had lost them. Thompson darted out and managed to pick Props up again. He spent the time wandering about the streets, but always drawing nearer this part of the world. Just before Thompson rang up, Props had led him into the jumble of streets round the back of the Unicorn. He kept him in sight until he turned up a cul-de-sac called Simon's Alley. Thompson followed and came to a gate leading into a yard. He looked round and decided that he was somewhere at the back of the theatre. He climbed the gate and found an open window that he believes gives into some part of the Unicorn. It was pitch-dark inside. Thompson was in a quandary. He decided to call me. First of all he managed to find one of our men and told him what he'd seen. That took some time. The man hailed a constable and left him in his place while he himself came round to the gate. That took longer. Thompson, whom Allah preserve, for I won't, prowled round on a Cook's tour in search of a telephone and finally rang me up. Lord knows how long the gate was left unguarded. Quite five minutes, I should say, if not longer."

"Well, sir, whatever Props was up to it would probably take longer than that."

"Yes. Of course it was difficult for Thompson. He didn't want to start blowing his whistle and the gaff at the same time. Now here's where we get out and grope for Simon's Alley. I'll just see the others first."

They left the car and went back a little way to where a second police car was drawn up. Alleyn gave instructions to the six constables who were in it. They were to split up singly, go to the several doors of the theatre, and enter it, leaving the men already on guard in their places.

"I don't know what we'll find," said Alleyn, "but I expect it'll be in the stage half of the theatre. You four come quietly through the stalls, from the several doors, and wait by the orchestra well. Don't use your torches unless you've got to. You come in at the back entrance, and at the stage door. Don't make a move until you get the word from Inspector Fox or myself. If you meet anything, grab it. Right?"

"Right, sir."

"Away you go then. Come on, Fox."

They had pulled up some little way from the back of the Unicorn. Alleyn led the way through a confused jumble of by-streets into the dingy thoroughfare behind the theatre. At last they came into a very narrow, blind street. Alleyn pointed up at the corner building and Fox read the notice: "Simon's Alley."

They walked quietly along the left-hand pavement. The roof of the Unicorn, looking gigantic, cut across the night-blue sky. No one was abroad in Simon's Alley and the traffic of Piccadilly and Trafalgar Square sounded remote. They heard Big Ben strike eleven. In a little while they saw the figure of a man standing very still in the shadows. Alleyn waited until he had come up with him.

"'Is that you, Thompson?" he said very quietly.

"Yes, sir. I'm sorry if I've gone wrong over this."

"Not altogether your fault, but it would have been better if you'd kept your relief with you. Sure Hickson went in here?"

"Yes, sir. I had to leave this gate unwatched while I got the constable to come round. It's a long way round, too, but it wasn't more than eight minutes. I hope Hickson's still inside."

"Stay here. Don't move unless you hear my whistle. Come on, Fox."

He put his foot on the gate handle and climbed up. For a moment his silhouette showed dark against the sky. Then he disappeared. Fox followed him. The yard was strewn with indistinguishable rubbish. They picked their way cautiously towards the wall in front of them, and turned a corner, where the yard narrowed into an alley-way behind a low building. Here they found the open window. Alleyn noticed the old and broken shutter and the hole in the pane that would allow access to the catch. With a mental shrug at the watchman's idea of a burglar-proof theatre, Alleyn put his hands on the sill, wriggled through, and waited for Fox, who soon stood beside him. They took off their shoes and stayed there in the dark, listening.

Alleyn's eyes became accustomed to the murk; he saw that they were in a small lumber-room of sorts, that its only door stood open, and that there was a wall beyond. The place smelt disused and dank. He switched on his torch for a moment. From the room they went into a narrow stone passage, up half a dozen steps and through another door. They took a right-angled turn and passed a row of doors, all of them locked. The passage turned again and grew lighter. Alleyn touched Fox on the hand and pointed to the side and then forward. Fox nodded. They were in country they knew. These were the dressing-rooms. They moved now with the utmost caution and came to the elbow in the passage where Alleyn and Nigel had met Simpson on the night of the murder. There was Gardener's dressing-room and there on the door beyond it hung the tarnished star. A thin flood of light met them. Props had turned on a lamp, somewhere beyond, where the stage was. Alleyn crept forward hugging the wall. He held up his hand. From somewhere out on the stage came a curious sound. It was a kind of faint sibilation as of two surfaces that brushed together, parted, brushed together again. They stayed very still, listening to this whisper, and presently thought it was accompanied by the echo of a creak.

"Scenery," breathed Fox. "Hanging."

"Perhaps."

Alleyn edged down the passage until he could see part of the stage. Nothing stirred. It was very ill-lit out there. He thought what light there was must come from the pilot-lamp above the book in the prompt corner. They waited again for some minutes. Alleyn could see through one of the stage entrances that the curtain was up. Beyond, in the darkness, two of his men must be waiting. Round on his left in the stage door passage, yet another man stood and listened, and a fourth had come in at the back door and was motionless, somewhere in the shadows across the stage. He knew they must all be there, as silent as himself and as silent as Props.

At last he went out on to the stage. He went to the stage door passage and stood there, knowing his man must see him against the light. Presently a hand touched his arm.

"Nobody here or in the dock, sir."

Fox was out on the stage and had crossed through the wings. Alleyn gave him a few minutes longer, and then made his way to the prompt corner. He went out by the footlights, where he knew the men in the stalls would see him. He pointed his torch out into the house and switched it on. A face leapt out of the dark and blinked. One of his own men. He hunted round the stage which was set as he had left it. His stocking foot trod on a piece of glass that must have been left there from the broken chandelier. All this time the faint, sibilant noise and the intermittent creak persisted. He now realised that they came from above his head.

Perhaps Props was back in his perch up there in the grid. Perhaps he waited with a rope in his hands ready to loose another bulk of dead weight. But why should Props let that noise go on up there? There was no draught of air.

From the centre of the stage Alleyn spoke aloud. He was conscious of a dread to hear his own voice. When it came it sounded strange.

"Fox!" he said. "Where are you?"

"Here, sir." Fox was over near the prompt corner.

"Get up that little iron ladder to the switchboard. If he's here he's lying low. Give us all the light in the house. I refuse to play sardines with Mr. Hickson."

Fox climbed the ladder slowly. From down in front one of the constables gave a deprecatory cough.

Click. Click.

The circle came into view, then the stalls. The constables were standing in the two aisles.

Click.

The footlights sprang up in a white glare. Then the proscenium was cinctured with warmth. The lamp on the stage suddenly came alive. The passages glowed. A blaze of light sprang up above the stage. The theatre was awake.

In the centre of the stage Alleyn stood with his eyes screwed up, blinded by light. The two constables came through the wings, their hands arched over their faces. From the switchboard Fox said:

"That's light enough to see an invisible man."

Alleyn, still peering, bent over the footlights. "You

two in front," he said, "search the place thoroughly—offices upstairs—cloak-rooms—everything. We'll deal with this department."

He turned to the men on the stage.

"We'll go about this in pairs. He's a shell-shocked man and he's a bit desperate. Somewhere or another in this rabbit warren he's hidden. I think he'll be in his own department behind the scenes. We'll wait till these fellows in the front of the house come back."

They lit cigarettes and stayed uneasily on the stage. The sound of doors shutting announced the activities of the men in front.

"Rum sort of place this, when there's nothing doing." said Fox.

"Yes," Alleyn agreed. "It feels expectant."

"Any idea why he came here, sir?"

"Unfortunately I have. A particularly nasty idea."

The others waited hopefully.

Alleyn stubbed his cigarette on the floor.

"I think he had a rendezvous," he said. "With a murderer."

Fox looked scandalised and perturbed.

"Or murderess as the case may be," added Alleyn.

"Cuh!" said one of the plain-clothes men under his breath.

"But," said Fox, "they're all under surveillance."

"I know. Thompson's man gave him the slip. There may be another of our wonderful police who's lost his sheep and doesn't know where to find it. Not a comfortable thought, but it arises. What's the time?"

"Eleven-twenty, sir."

"What the devil is that whispering noise?" asked Alleyn restively. He peered up into the flies. A ceiling-cloth was stretched across under the lowest gallery and the grids were hidden.

"I noticed something of the sort the night of the murder," said Fox. "There must be a draught up there making the canvas swing a bit."

Apparently Alleyn did not hear him. He walked across to the ladder by which Props had descended. He stood there, very still, for a moment. When he spoke his voice sounded oddly.

"I think," he said, "we will begin with the grid."

The two men returned from the front of the house. Alleyn walked over to the proscenium door, which was locked. The key hung on a nail beside it. He opened the door. It emitted a loud shriek.

"So much for Bathgate's theory," murmured Alleyn.

The men came through.

"Wait here," said Alleyn. "I'm going into the grid."

"Not on your own, sir," chided Fox. "That chap may be sitting there ready to dong you one."

"I think not. Follow me up if you like."

He climbed the iron ladder that ran flat up the wall. Slowly the shadow of the ceiling-cloth enfolded him. Fox followed.

The other four men stood with their faces tipped back, watching. Alleyn's stocking feet disappeared above the ceiling-cloth. The ladder vibrated slightly.

"Wait a moment, Fox."

Alleyn's voice sounded eerily above their heads. Fox paused.

Alleyn's dulled footsteps thumped on the gallery overhead. The cloth quivered and sagged. He had unloosed the ropes that fastened it. Presently, with a sort of swishing sigh, the border fell away and the whole thing collapsed in a cloud of dust on to the tops of the wings.

When the dust had settled, the men who looked upwards saw the soles of a pair of rubber shoes. The shoes turned slowly to the right, stopped, turned slowly to the left. The canvas having been taken away they no longer fretted it with a sibilant whisper, but every time they swung, the rope round Prop's neck creaked on the wooden cleat above.

Chapter XXI

THIS INEFFABLE EFFRONTERY

Inspector Fox was accustomed to what he termed unpleasantness, but for a moment he nearly lost his grip on the iron ladder.

"Props," he said slowly. "So Props was the man, after all."

"Come up here," said Alleyn.

They stood together on the first gallery. Their faces were on a level with the shoulders of the swinging body. The rope that had hanged him was a slack end of the pulley that had suspended the chandelier. It was made fast to a cleat on the top gallery. Fox leant out and touched the hand.

"He's still warm."

"It happened," said Alleyn, "just before Thompson rang up the Yard."

He stood with his hands clenched to the rail of the gallery, gazing, as if against his will, at the body.

"I should have prevented this," he said. "I should have made the arrest this afternoon."

"I don't see that," said Fox in his ponderous way. "How could you have foretold——"

"This ineffable effrontery," finished Alleyn. "Poor Props."

"That sort's very liable to suicide."

"Suicide?" Alleyn turned to him. "This is not suicide."

"Not——?"

"It's murder. Come up to the gallery here."

They climbed the upper length of ladder. Alleyn paused when his head and shoulders were above the top gallery and switched on his torch.

"Swept!" he said, with a kind of triumph. "Now, my beauty—I've got you!"

"What's that, sir?" asked Fox from below.

"The gallery's been swept. Do suicides tidy up the ground when they set about it? Thick dust farther along. The typewriter was too tidy and so's this gallows. There'll be no prints, but the mark of the criminal is all over it. We can take the body down now, Fox. I'll stay here a moment. You go back."

They had to draw the body in to the first gallery and then get it down the ladder—no easy job. At last Props lay on the stage in his accustomed surroundings. In answer to Fox's whistle the others had come in from the doors. Thompson was white about the gills and couldn't speak. Alleyn turned to him.

"We've had ill luck to-day, Thompson," he said. "I should have made more sure of him."

"It's my fault, sir."

"No," said Alleyn; "the poor devil was too quick for you."

"I still don't see how it was worked."

"Suppose I said I'd meet you here. Suppose I'd killed a man and you knew it. I get here first. I go up there to the platform, put a noose in that rope, and make the other end fast. Then I climb down again. You come in, very nervous. You've been followed, you say, but you've shaken them off. We start to talk. Then I say I can hear someone coming along that passage. 'By God, they're after us,' I say. 'Come on up this ladder. Quick.' I go up first, past the lower landing. He follows. I get to the top landing and wait with the noose in my hands. As his head come up, I drop it over. One fierce tug. He loosens his hands and claws his neck. Then a heavy thrust and—— That's how it worked."

"My oath!" said Fox.

"Yes, but I've left a broom up there because I know my stockinged feet will leave prints in the dust—the thick dust. So while Props is jerking in the air I sweep away the dust. He's hidden by the ceiling cloth. He won't be missed until to-morrow. It's an old building—some more dust will have fallen then. They may not find him at once, and if they do it looks like suicide. So I take the broom down with me and leave it on the stage in its usual place. Then I run down those nightmare passages into the little store-room. Thompson is in the yard outside. I wait. Presently I hear him go off to get his man from the front of the theatre. That's my chance. When he comes back—I'm not there."

"I see," said Fox heavily. "Yes. I see."

"Now, look here." Alleyn bent over the body. "The head and shoulders are covered in dust. It was there while he was still hanging. It was swept off the top gallery. Analysis will prove it. We've got to come all over scientific, Fox."

"It can't be Saint and it wasn't Props. That's two people cleared away in favour of your theory, sir."

"It is."

"What do we do now, then?"

"Get hold of the men who were watching the rest of the party."

"I'll ring up the Yard. Reports should have come through by now."

"Yes," said Alleyn. "Do that, Fox. I'm especially anxious for the report from Cambridge."

"Yes."

"And from—who's that fellow? Oh, Detective-Sergeant Watkins. Find out if he's been relieved, and if he has tell them to get hold of him and send him round here."

"Very good, sir."

"And ring up Bailey. He'll be in bed now, poor creature, but we'll have to beat him up. And the divisional surgeon. Oh, Lord—here we go again."

Fox disappeared through the proscenium door. Alleyn went back along the stone passages. He turned up the lights and examined the floor and walls carefully. He walked, hugging the wall, all the way to the room with the broken window. Here he examined the floor, the walls, the window-sill and the yard outside. He turned his torch on the gate, climbed it, and scrutinsed the top meticulously. Here he found a tiny scrap of black cloth which he preserved.

Then he returned to the stage.

He shook some of the dust from Prop's hair into an

envelope, sealed it up, and, taking a fresh envelope, turned his attention to the shoulders of the coat. He climbed the ladder to the top gallery, where he took a further sample of dust. Using his pocket-lens and his torch he examined the rope carefully, paying particular attention to the noose and the three or four feet above it. He also scrutinized the rail and floor of the gallery for some distance beyond the place where the ladder came up. He then measured the length of the drop. Returning to the stage he found a broom under the electrician's gallery, and from this also he obtained a specimen of dust. He examined the body, paying particular attention to the hands. Bailey and the divisional surgeon arrived while he was still about this business.

"You'll find no prints except his," said Alleyn.

The surgeon made his examination.

"I hear the verdict is murder," he said. "I don't know your reading of it, inspector, but he died from strangulation and a broken neck. I can see no signs of anything else, except a slight bruise at the base of the neck."

"Could that have been caused by a downward kick from a stockinged foot?" Alleyn asked.

"Yes," said the surgeon. He looked up to where the iron ladder ran into the galleries. "I see," he said.

"What about Watkins?"

Fox, who had returned to the stage, answered:

"He'd gone home but they are turning him out."

"Any news from Cambridge?"

"A long statement from a servant at Peterhouse. They're sending it round with the officer who went down there. The mortuary van's here."

"Right. They can come in now."

Fox went to the stage door and returned followed by two men with a stretcher.

Props was carried out of the Unicorn at exactly midnight.

"I feel like Hamlet when he killed Polonius," said Alleyn.

"Shakespeare," said Fox. "I don't read that sort of thing myself."

But the surgeon stood on the stage and said quietly:
"'Thou wretched, rash, intruding fool, farewell.' I suppose the words have been spoken here before," he reflected.

"Under somewhat different circumstances," said Alleyn harshly.

"Here's Watkins," said Fox.

Detective-Sergeant Watkins was a stocky, sandy-headed man. He looked worried.

"You want to see me, sir?" he said to Alleyn.

"I want an account of your day, Watkins."

"Very monotonous it was really. The party I was looking after stayed indoors from the time I relieved until the time I came off."

"Are you sure of that?"

Watkins flushed.

"I sat on a bench in the gardens opposite and I stood by the lamp-post. I never took my eyes off the door, sir."

"Who passed in and out?"

"Other people in the building. I saw my party several times—looked out of the window."

"When was the last time you noted that?"

"At fifteen minutes to ten, sir," said Watkins triumphantly.

"Who came out of the building after that?"

"Quite a number of people, sir. Going out for supper-parties and so on. I recognised most of them as residents."

"Any that you did not recognise?"

"There was a woman. Looked like a working woman, I thought, and a couple of housemaids, and before them an old gentleman in a soft hat and a dinner suit and a sort of opera cloak. He was a bit lame. The commissionaire got him a taxi. I heard him say 'The Plaza Theatre' to the driver. I asked the commissionaire about them just to be on the safe side. He's a dense sort of bloke. He thought the woman must have been doing odd work in one of the flats. The old gent he didn't know, but said he came from the top floor, and had probably been dining there. The housemaids came from the street-level flat."

"That's all?"

"No, sir. One other. A young fellow wearing a shepherd's plaid double-breasted suit, a bowler hat, and a dark blue tie with pale blue stripes, came along. I crossed the street and heard him name our party's floor to the liftman."

"Had he a fair moustache and a carnation in his coat?"

"Yes, sir."

"Did he reappear?" Alleyn asked sharply.

"He came out again after about five minutes and walked off towards the square. That's all, sir. I was relieved at ten-fifteen by Detective-Sergeant Allison. He's still on duty."

"Thank you. That's all, Watkins."

"Have I gone wrong anywhere, sir?"

"Yes. You've mistaken a murderer for an innocent person. I don't know that I blame you. Get one of these men to relieve Allison and ask him to report here immediately."

Watkins said nothing, but looked miserable. He and Thompson conferred sympathetically. After a few moments Watkins said diffidently:

"If I may, sir, I'd like to relieve Allison myself."

"Very well, Watkins. If anybody comes away from the building, man or woman, stop them, speak to them, get their names and addresses and make sure they are what they seem. Thompson, you can go too if you like. Don't look so injured, both of you. We've all gone wrong over this."

A pause, and then Thompson addressed the lining of his hat with some feeling.

"We'd both go back on P.C. night-duty before we'd let you down, if you know what I mean, sir."

"That's right," said Watkins fervently.

"Well, push off, you couple of boobies," said Alleyn. He turned to Fox. "I'm going to the telephone. The statement from Peterhouse ought to be here any moment. If Allison comes before I'm back, get a report on those lines from him."

"Are you going for a warrant-to-arrest to-night?" asked Fox.

"I don't think so. I'll still stage my performance to-morrow morning."

Alleyn went through the front of the house and sought out the telephone in the box-office. Enlargements of actresses smiled or stared soulfully at him from the walls. "All the best," "To dear Robert," "Ever yours," he read. In the centre was a magnificent picture of a woman standing in an open window. Written firmly across the mount were two words only: "Stephanie Vaughan." When he had dialled his number Alleyn turned and gazed steadfastly at this picture.

"Hullo!" said a sleepy voice in the receiver.

"Hullo. I thought I said there were to be no more little visits."

"Oh—it's you."

"It is," said Alleyn grimly.

"I had an idea. You needn't get all hot and bothered, I didn't see anybody. I rang for five minutes and then came away. Even the servant was out."

"You rang for five minutes, did you?"

"Yes. I say, is everything all right?"

"Perfectly splendid. There been another murder at the Unicorn."

"What! !"

"Go to bed and stay there," advised Alleyn and hung up the receiver.

He crossed over and looked more closely at the photograph on the opposite wall.

"Oh, hell!" he said and went back to the stage of the Unicorn.

Chapter XXII

FINAL CURTAIN

On the morning of June 17th, at a quarter to eleven, old Blair hung his dilapidated bowler above the tall stool in his cubby-hole behind the stage door. He glanced at the grimy clock and clicked disapproval when he saw that it had been allowed to run down. He inspected the letter rack which was garnished with a solitary postcard, addressed to Miss Susan Max. Blair advanced his nose to within four inches of its surface and read it :

Susan darling, how terrible this all is dear my heart goes out to you in this terrible time it must be quite dreadful for you dear, our show goes big in this place and we are doing wonderful business dear. All the best, Daisy.

Blair sucked his teeth, but whether in scorn or appreciation it would be impossible to say.

Footsteps sounded in the alley outside. Old Blair groaned slightly and returned to the stage door. The constable at the stalls entrance saluted. Chief Detective-Inspector Alleyn and Inspector Fox followed by Detective-Sergeant Bailey and three plain clothes men walked up to the entrance.

" Good morning, Blair," said Alleyn.

" 'Morning, sir."

The party went in at the stage door and down the long passage past the wall of the dock. On the stage they were met by two more plain clothes men—Thompson and Watkins.

" Everything fixed up?" asked Alleyn.

" Yes, sir."

Alleyn looked up towards the flies. A ceiling-cloth had been stretched across and tied back to the first of the grid galleries.

" If you'll just listen, sir," said Thompson.

They all stood still. A sibilant whisper came from above the canvas cloth. It alternated with a faint creak. At a place near its border, the cloth bulged slightly as if some small object was touching it on the upper surface. The impress made by this object appeared and disappeared regularly, synchronising with the sibilant whisper.

"That will do very well," said Alleyn. "Have you unlocked the dressing-room doors"

Apparently this had been done. Alleyn went on to the stage and glanced round. It was still set for the scene when Surbonadier loaded the revolver. The curtain was up and the shrouded seats looked very faint in the dark. A lance of sunlight slanted through a crevice in a blind above the gallery. Footsteps sounded in the passage and Mr. George Simpson appeared. He looked nervously round the wings, saw Alleyn, and uttered a little apologetic noise.

"Oh, there you are, Mr. Simpson," said Alleyn. "I've been trying to pretend I'm a stage manager. Any fault to find with the scene?"

Simpson walked down to the float and surveyed the stage. Something of his professional manner seemed to return to the little man.

"It's quite in order, I think," he said.

"Perhaps I'd better wait until the company appears before I explain my motive in calling you all this morning."

"Some of them are outside now."

"Right. Will you treat Detective-Sergeants Wilkins as your call-boy? As soon as everybody's here we'll have them on the stage and I'll speak to them."

Sergeant Wilkins was produced. He and Simpson eyed each other doubtfully.

"What's that you've got in your hand, Wilkins?" asked Alleyn suddenly.

"It's one of your cards, sir. The young gentleman I saw yesterday, if you remember, sir, came along. He just wanted to sit in the stalls."

"Let me see it."

Alleyn surveyed, rather grimly his own visiting-card with: "Admit bearer to theatre. R.A." scribbled across it in his own writing. It was the one he had given Nigel before they arrested Saint. With remarkable forethought Mr. Bathgate had clung to the bit of pasteboard and had produced it again when the occasion arose.

With a slightly accentuated jaw-line, Inspector Alleyn advanced to the footlights and gazed into the swimming darkness of the stalls.

" Mr. Bathgate," he said.

Silence.

" Mr. Bathgate," lied Alleyn, " I can see you."

" You're not looking in my direction at all," declared an indignant voice.

" Come here," Alleyn said.

" I won't."

" If you please."

There was a mulish silence and then Alleyn said mildly :
" House lights, Mr. Simpson, if you please."

Simpson scuttled up the iron ladder and in a moment the stalls were revealed in all their shrouded grimness.

In the centre of Row F, a lonely little figure among the dust sheets, sat Nigel. Alleyn beckoned. Nigel rose sheepishly and processed down the centre aisle.

" Now," said Alleyn, when the culprit reached the curtain of the well. " Now, my enterprising Pressman."

Nigel smirked but did not reply.

" I've a good mind to have you turfed out at the end of a boot," continued Alleyn. He looked seriously at Nigel. " However, I won't do that. I will merely return my card with an additional memorandum. If you still want to stay here you may."

He wrote something on the back of the card and flipped it across the orchestra well.

Nigel caught it and held it to the light. Inspector Alleyn wrote in tiny but exceedingly clear characters, yet, though there were only seven words on the card, Nigel appeared to take an unconscionable time deciphering them. At last he raised his head and he and Alleyn looked at each other.

" It's a mistake," said Nigel.

" No."

"But——" He stopped short and wetted his lips. "No motive," said Nigel at last.

"Every motive."

"I'll stay," said Nigel.

"Very well. House lights, please, Mr. Simpson."

Once again the front of the house was dark.

"I think they are all here now, Inspector Alleyn," said Simpson nervously.

"Ask them to come here, will you, Wilkins?" said Alleyn.

The company of *The Rat and the Beaver* reassembled for the last time on the stage of the Unicorn. They came down the passage in single file. Susan Max and Stephanie Vaughan appeared first. Then came Janet Emerald walking with the gait she used in the provinces for the last act of *Madam X.* Dulcie Deamer followed, expressing tragic bewilderment. Next came Felix Gardener, very white-faced and alone. Howard Melville and J. Barclay Crammer delayed their entrance and made it arm-in-arm with heads held high, like French aristocrats approaching the tumbrels.

"Everybody on the stage, please," said George Simpson.

The players walked through the wings and stood quietly in a semi-circle. They looked attentive and business-like. It was almost as though they had needed the stage and the lights to give them full solidity. They no longer seemed preposterous or even artificial. They were in their right environment and had become real.

Alleyn stood down by the float, facing the stage. From the auditorium, with the full stage lighting behind him, it was he who now looked a strange shadow, but for the actors there was no suggestion of this; to them he was in the accustomed place of the producer, and they watched him attentively.

"Ladies and gentlemen," said Alleyn, "I have asked you to come here this morning in order that we may stage a reconstruction of the first scene in the last act of *The Rat and the Beaver*. In that scene, as you know the deceased man, Mr. Arthur Surbonadier, loaded the revolver by which he was subsequently shot. You are all aware that Mr. Jacob Saint is under arrest. He will not be present. Otherwise, with the exception of the deceased, whose part will be read by Mr. Simpson, we are all here."

He paused for a moment. The stage manager looked as though he wanted to say something.

"Yes, Mr. Simpson?"

"Er—I don't know if it matters. The property master has not turned up. As he gave me the dummies I thought perhaps——?"

"We shall have to do without him," said Alleyn. "Are the dressers here?"

Simpson glanced offstage. Beadle and Trixie Beadle came through the wings and stood awkwardly at the end of the semi-circle.

"First I must tell you, all of you, that the police have formed a definite theory as regards this crime. It is in order to substantiate this theory that the reconstruction is necessary. I want to impress upon you that, apart from its distressing associations, there is nothing to worry about in the business. I merely ask the innocent members of the company to rehearse a particular scene in order to verify my theory as regards the movements of the guilty individual. I most earnestly beg of you to behave exactly as you did, so far as you can remember, during the last performance of this scene. I give you this opportunity to vindicate yourselves and at the same time establish the case which we shall bring before the court. I appeal to you to play fair. As innocent individuals you have nothing to fear. Is it agreed?"

He waited for a moment and then Barclay Crammer cleared his throat portentously. He advanced two places and gazed into the auditorium.

"I do not know if Miss Vaughan or Mr. Gardener have anything to say——" he began.

"Nothing," said Stephanie Vaughan quickly. "I'm quite ready to do it."

"I too," said Gardener.

"In that case," continued Mr. Crammer deeply, "I may say at once that I am prepared to play out this horrible farce—to the end." He let his voice break slightly. "God grant we may be the instruments to avenge poor Arthur." He made a slight gesture expressive of noble resignation and very nearly bowed to the empty auditorium. The hidden Nigel refrained, with something of an effort, from giving him a heartfelt clap. Alleyn caught Gardener's eye. Gardener looked as though he wanted to wink.

"That's all settled, then," said Alleyn. "Now the only difference between this and the real show is that I am not going to black-out the lights. I will ask those of you who were in your dressing-rooms at the end of the interval to go to them. Any movement that you made from one room to another you will repeat. You will see that I have stationed officers along the passages. Please behave exactly as if they were not there. The conversation on the stage between Miss Max, Mr. Surbonadier, Miss Emerald, and Mr. Simpson before the curtain went up, we will reproduce as closely as possible. I will blow the whistle at the point when you are to imagine the black-out takes place, and again when the lights would go on. Now will you all go to your dressing-rooms?"

They filed off quietly. Simpson went to the prompt box and Sergeant Wilkins joined him there.

Alleyn had a word with both of them. Fox and Bailey stood offstage by the first and third left entrances. Two other men went to the O.P. Thompson and a third man disappeared down the dressing-room passage.

"Right," said Alleyn, and walked down to the float.

"Call the last act, please," said Simpson to Sergeant Wilkins.

Wilkins went off down the dressing-room passage. His voice could be heard on the stage.

"Last act, please, last act, please!"

Miss Max, who dressed in a room round the elbow of the passage, came out first, walked on to the stage, sat in the chair on the O.P. side and took out her knitting. She was followed by Janet Emerald who went straight to the upstage window.

"Stay there as if you were speaking to Surbonadier," said Alleyn quietly. "Now, Mr. Simpson."

Simpson came out of the prompt box and went to the desk. He mimed the business of putting something in the top drawer.

"Now, Miss Emerald," said Alleyn.

"I don't remember—what I said."

"About the cartridges dear," said Miss Max quietly.

"*I—I'm always afraid you'll forget those cartridges.*" said Janet Emerald.

"*Trust little Georgie,*" said Simpson.

"*George, come over here. I want to show you something. This mat is bad where it is, dear.*"

"*What's wrong with the mat, Susan?*"

"*It jams the door and spoils my eggzit.*"

"*Is that better?*"

"*That's where it should be. Come here and let me measure my scarf.*"

"Now, Miss Emerald, you spoke to Surbonadier."

"I—I can't. It's too horrible."

"Go across to the left and meet Mr. Simpson. You say: "Arthur's tight, George, and I'm nervous.""

"*Arthur's tight, George, and I'm nervous.*"

"*He's giving a damn' good show, anyway.*"

"Now you whisper: 'I'd like to kill him,' and stand with your hands on the desk."

"*I'd—like—to kill——*"

"*All clear, please.*"

Janet Emerald stood up and faced upstage.

"*House lights. Stand by, please. Black-out.*"

Alleyn blew a long blast on his whistle. Simpson with the book in his hand went on to the stage. Alleyn stood in the wings, where he could see the stage and dressing-room passage. Melville, who had stood near the prompt box, went tiptoe down the passage and round the elbow. Miss Vaughan came out of her room, leaving the door open; she knocked on Gardener's door. He called; "Come in," and she entered, closing the door behind her. It reopened to let out old Beadle. He stood outside,

179

produced a cigarette and held it, unlit, in his mouth. Trixie Beadle came out of the star-room and joined him. They moved into the elbow of the passage.

Felix Gardener came out of his room and walked softly on to the stage. Here he paused, started, bent down and rubbed his foot, whispered: "What the hell!" and limped on a few paces. The Beadles walked away down the passage towards the wardrobe-room. All this took a very short space of time. On the stage Simpson called: "Curtain up." The actors began to speak the dialogue, muttering their lines and raising their voices loudly at the end of each speech. This dialogue continued for perhaps half a minute and then the stage manager said:

"*Lights.*"

Alleyn blew his whistle and called out:

"Everyone on the stage, please."

Once more the company assembled.

"Thank you very much," said Alleyn. "You have helped me. I am sure it has been difficult and unpleasant for all of you. I can now explain myself a little further. I think you are entitled to an explanation. This reconstruction has proved that no one, who was beyond the elbow in the passage, could have come out on to the stage without running into the two dressers, who did not go to the wardrobe-room until late in the black-out period. Mr. Gardener has stated that when he went on to the stage someone trod on his foot. There are only three men who could have been offstage at that time—Mr. Simpson, the property master—and Mr. Jacob Saint."

Janet Emerald began some sort of demonstration. Alleyn glanced coldly at her and she subsided.

"Mr. Saint was in his box on the prompt side. One theory was that he came through the proscenium door, substituted the cartridges, and returned by the same route. Wilkins, will you go to that door, open it and walk to the desk?"

Sergeant Wilkins marched to the proscenium exit and opened the door. It gave tongue to an ear-splitting shriek.

"That disposes of that," said Alleyn. "Mr. Simpson

and Props are left. The theory as regards Props is this. Props was on the stage during the black-out. He substituted the cartridges, and then made himself scarce. No one remembered seeing him offstage when the lights went up. Where did he go? The theory suggests that he went up that ladder and disappeared above the ceiling-cloth. If you'll be good enough to help me I'll demonstrate that. Mr. Simpson is in the prompt box; Miss Max, Miss Emerald, and the deceased are on the stage. Mr. Gardener comes out of the passage and runs into Props, who has just planted the cartridges. He shies off Mr. Gardener and goes up that ladder. He is wearing rubber shoes and is not heard. He wears Mr. Saint's gloves that were left on the stage. Now, Mr. Simpson, will you be good enough to play his part?"

Simpson wetted his lips.

"I—I can't stand going up those ladders. I've no head for heights. It would—make—— I can't."

Alleyn looked doubtfully at the bulk of Crammer and the greenish face of Mr. Melville. He turned resignedly to Gardener.

"Be a good fellow," he said.

"Certainly," said Gardener quietly.

"If your nerves will allow you, Mr. Simpson, perhaps you will impersonate Mr. Gardner."

Simpson did not speak.

"Surely you can do that?"

"I'll do it," said Melville.

"Thank you—I should prefer Mr. Simpson to play this little scene. Now, Mr. Simpson."

Simpson turned and went into Gardener's room.

"Away you go," said Alleyn to Gardener, who nodded and went to the desk. He drew out the top drawer, mimed the business of taking something out, putting something else in. He opened the lower drawer and shut it again, hesitated, glanced interrogatively at Alleyn, and came back to the wings.

"Come out. Mr. Simpson," called Alleyn.

The dressing-room door opened and Simpson came out. He walked down the passage and on to the stage.

Gardener bumped into him, stepped aside and began to climb the ladder.

"Right up?" he asked.

"Yes, please."

Gardener went on up the ladder. They watched him. Suddenly they were all aware of the sibilant whisper and of the moving indentation in the cloth. His steps rang on the iron rungs. His head disappeared above the cloth. Then a terrible cry rang out.

"My God, what's that!" screamed Simpson.

Gardener's body swung out from the ladder. It seemed as if he would fall. His feet slipped and for a moment he hung by his hands. Then he righted himself.

"Alleyn!" he cried in a terrible voice, "Alleyn!"

"What's the matter?" shouted Alleyn.

"He's here—he's hanged himself—he's here."

"Who?"

"Props—it's Props."

His horrified face looked down at them.

"It's Props!" he repeated.

Fox, Bailey, Wilkins and Thompson came and stood by the foot of the ladder.

"Come down," said Alleyn.

Gardener came down. Within six rungs of the stage he turned and saw the men that awaited him. With an incoherent cry he stopped short. His lips were drawn back, showing his gums. A streak of saliva trickled down his chin. He squinted.

"And how do you know it is Props?" asked Alleyn.

Gardener kicked down savagely at his face.

"Not again," said Alleyn. "The other time was once too often."

Fox had to drag Gardener down by his ankles. This time Alleyn had remembered his handcuffs.

Chapter XXIII

EPILOGUE TO A PLAY

If Chief Detective-Inspector Alleyn was interested in the dramatic unities it may have given him some sort of satisfaction to note that the epilogue to the Unicorn murder was spoken on the stage of the theatre.

Gardener had been taken away. Miss Emerald had indulged in a fit of genuine hysterics and had departed. Barclay Crammer, George Simpson, Howard Melville and Dulcie Deamer, all strangely unreal in the harsh light of actual tragedy, had walked down the stage door alley-way and disappeared. The Beadles had gone with old Blair.

Only Alleyn, Stephanie Vaughan, and a very shaken Nigel remained. The ceiling-cloth had been removed and the weighted sack that had hung from the top gallery lay in a rubbishy heap on the floor. Alleyn picked it up, and threw it into the dock, and shut the doors. Nigel stood in the stage door passage. Alleyn looked at him.

"Well, Bathgate," he said. "Never make friends with a policeman."

"I don't think I feel that way about it," decided Nigel slowly.

"You are generous," said Alleyn.

"Why didn't you tell me?"

"If I had told you what would you have done?"

Nigel couldn't answer that.

"I don't know," he said.

"Neither did I know."

"I see."

"Did the thought of it never enter your head?" Alleyn asked him compassionately.

"At first I thought it was Saint and then——" He looked through the wings on to the stage.

Stephanie Vaughan sat there in the arm-chair she had

occupied on the night of the murder when Alleyn had first questioned her. She seemed lost in a profound meditation.

"Wait for me," said Alleyn, "somewhere else."

Nigel walked out into the yard. Alleyn went on to the stage.

"Come back from wherever you are," he said softly.

She raised her head and looked at him.

"I can't feel anything at all," she murmured.

He put his hand over hers for a second.

"Cold," he said. "That's the shock. Whenever I have touched your hands they have been cold. Small wonder. Shall I get you a taxi?"

"Not yet. I want to get my bearings."

She looked frowningly at her fingers as though she tried to remember something.

"I suppose you knew what I was up to all along?" she said at last.

"Not quite. I began to wonder, when you said the bruise on your shoulder was made by Surbonadier. I remembered how Gardener had stood with his hand on your shoulder when Surbonadier insulted you. I noticed how he gripped you."

She shivered.

"I was afraid then that he would do something dreadful," she said.

"If it's any comfort to you he would have done just what he did if you hadn't existed."

"I know. I was only an accessory after the fact, isn't it? At any rate, not a motive."

"In Surbonadier's flat," Alleyn told her, "I knew how much you were prepared to risk for him. I let you play your part. I let you think you had succeeded."

"Why do you rub it in?"

"Why, to put it rather floridly, because I thought it would help you to hate me and so provide a counter-irritant."

"Oh," she said thoughtfully, "I don't hate you."

"That's strange."

"You were far too clever for me."

"And yet," said Alleyn, "half the victory is yours. From my heart I am sorry that it had to happen as it did. If I thought it would make any difference I would say I hated myself when I held you in my arms. It would only be half true. My thoughts were a mixture of grovel and glory."

"What will happen to him?" she said suddenly. Her eyes dilated.

"I don't know. He will be tried. He's guilty and he's a bad hat. You don't love him. Don't act. Don't pretend. It's going to be ghastly for you, but you left off loving him when you knew he'd done it."

"Yes, that's quite true."

She began to weep, not at all beautifully, but with her face screwed up and with harsh sobs. He looked gravely at her and when she put out her hand, put his handkerchief into it. He went to Surbonadier's dressing-room and found a nickel flask with whisky in it. With a grimace he washed a glass out and poured out a stiff nip. He took it back to her.

"Drink this. It'll pull you together."

She swallowed it, gasped, and shuddered.

"Now I'll get you a taxi," said Alleyn.

Nigel turned into the dock when he saw them come out. She got into the taxi.

"Good-bye," she said. "You know where to find me if—I'm wanted."

"Yes, you poor thing."

She held out her hand and, after a moment's hestitation, he kissed it.

"You'll recover," he told her. "Good-bye."

He gave the address to the driver and stood for some time in the empty yard. Then he went back to Nigel.

"Well?" he said. "What do you want to know?"

"Everything," said Nigel.

"All right. Lay back your ears, Here goes."

He pulled forward a couple of dingy arm-chairs and rolled back the doors of the dock, letting in a thin flood of sunshine.

"Here goes," he repeated and, lighting a cigarette, began his discourse.

"In homicide cases the police generally go for the obvious man. In spite of everything the psychologists say, and mind you they know what they're talking about, the obvious man is generally the 'he' in the game. In this case the obvious man was the one who pulled the trigger—Gardener. So from the first I considered him carefully. Would anyone else have risked planting the cartridges? Suppose Gardener had not pulled the trigger or had pulled it too soon? Would anyone else be likely to chance this? Well, they might. But If Gardener himself was the murderer he stood to risk nothing. The next thing I reminded myself of was the fact that I was up against good acting. Gardener was a consummately good actor. So I discounted all his remorse and bewilderment. How cleverly he talked about the insincerity of actors, quietly building up a picture of himself as the only genuine one amongst them. I deliberately refused to accept all this. When we took the statements from the others I noted at once that he and Stephanie Vaughan were nearest to the stage.

"At this time I was, of course, still watching everybody. But he was in his room with her and her room next door was unoccupied and close to the stage. How easy for him to dart in there when he left her, pull on Saint's gloves that he'd found on the stage (a stroke of luck that—he'd meant to use his own), make sure no one was in the passage, and then slip out, go on to the stage and in the dark change the cartridges. I wondered if his story of the sore foot was a fabrication, and deliberately I suggested the scent and he fell into the trap. That made me consider him seriously. Then he allowed you to get all that business about the libel case out of him, but only when he knew we'd find it out for ourselves. He told you Surbonadier had written the article. I wondered if he'd written it himself. When I found the forged signatures in Surbonadier's flat I felt sure Gardener had been the author. Suppose Surbonadier had blackmailed him, threatening to expose him

186

to Saint? Saint would have ruined his career. Suppose Surbonadier threatened to tell Stephanie Vaughan what I suspected was the truth about their Cambridge days? All supposition—but suggestive. I sent a man to Cambridge, who found the old servant who had looked after Gardener and who had overheard a conversation between him and Surbonadier in which Surbonadier accused him of writing the article. Gardener was much deeper in the drug-party stunts than he gave you to understand. No doubt his description of the passion he had for Stephanie Vaughan and the hatred he felt for Saint was true. This passion was drug-fed and inspired the article. I only got the Cambridge statement last night. It clinched matters.

"Then the wet-white. It was spilled after we left the dressing-room. Miss Vaughan said no one but herself and Trixie had been in the room after Surbonadier left it. Gardener was the only person who could have gone there. Anyone else would have run into the Beadles, who stood in the elbow of the passage before they went to the wardrobe-room. Gardener left her in his room to go to the stage. If Props had done the job he would not have gone near the star-room. Nor would Simpson, who was on the stage. Nor would Saint, if he'd come through the proscenium door, which squeaks like sour hell, anyway. But Gardener would."

"You mean," said Nigel, "he left her in his room, went into hers and put on the gloves, made sure there was no one in the passage and darted on to the stage. That was when he got the wet-white on the gloves?"

"Yes."

"What about the threatening letter?"

"Aha! His first bad break. He typed that letter on the stage during the last act for future use in case he wanted to substantiate that little romance of the sore toe. Then he must suddenly have remembered that after the murder he would probably be searched. He had prepared no plan to circumvent that; the whole business of the note was an impromptu effort suggested by his chance encounter in the dark. One imagines him regretting his cleverness then, for he couldn't possibly destroy the paper completely while on the stage. On the spur of the moment he must have slipped it out of sight somewhere about the desk, perhaps simply in the pile of unused type-paper. After I'd searched him he had the opportunity to retrieve it while he waited on the stage for Miss Vaughan. You told me he always hammered away at the letter Q in that scene. He must have remembered telling you that, and when he recovered the paper he wiped away the prints on the machine from every letter except Q. *Most* artistic, but fortunately Bailey had already tested the machine, careful creature that he is, and found Gardener's prints all over it. When we tested it again—no prints on any letter but Q. All would have been well if Bailey had been a little less industrious."

"But Stephanie Vaughan's confession——" began Nigel.

"Her confession! Her confession that she'd gone to Surbonadier's flat and tried to get back the forged paper that she knew he kept in his box. Her confession that I'd found her and she hoped she'd bamboozled me into thinking she was after her letters. Her confession that I'd held her in my arms and that I was his worst enemy——" Alleyn stopped short.

There was a long pause, during which Nigel gazed speculatively at his friend.

"And Props?" he said at last.

"Props I never suspected. A guilty man would never have blackguarded Surbonadier as he did and he was too silly, poor chap, to have done it. He had recognised Gardener somehow in the dark. He may have brushed against him and given him the idea of the toe tarradiddle. Quite possible. Anyway, Props was all for shielding the murderer of his girl's betrayer. Until he saw the news of Saint's arrest. Then he wrote that note to me. He rang up Gardener and I suppose told him he knew something. Gardener suggested the theatre as a rendezvous, probably Props mentioned the window in Simon's Alley.

Gardener dressed up as the old boy in an opera cloak and completely diddled our Mr. Wilkins. Disguise is usually a figment of detective fictionists' imagination, but again—Gardener was a consummate actor. He could risk it. You called while he was away murdering Props."

Alleyn described his views as regards the second murder. Nigel listened appalled.

"Wilkin's successor saw the old gentleman in the opera cloak return and failed to recognise him. The flat has been searched this morning. We hope to find evidence of the disguise. I think the overwhelming conceit of most murderers proved a little too much for Felix Gardener. The killing of Props was a bad mistake and yet—what could he do? Props, poor silly oaf that he was, evidently told him he wouldn't stand for an innocent man's trial and possible conviction. Props had to be got rid of. The method was not without points. If you hadn't called and found him out, if the old servant had not overheard that years-old conversation between himself and Surbonadier, if he hadn't got wet-white on his gloves—ah, well, there it is. We haven't been very clever. I'm handing no bouquets to myself over this case."

"Why did you want to get me out of the way?"

"My dear creature, because you were his friend, because he wondered how much you'd overheard in the flat, because—in short, because he's a murderer."

"I'm not convinced, Alleyn."

"You mean you don't want to be. It's perfectly beastly for you, I know. Were you greatly attached to him? Come now—were you?"

"I—well, perhaps not greatly attached, but we are by way of being friends."

"Where were you when I arrested him?"

"I had come round to the back. I stood under the electrician's platform."

"Then you saw him come down the ladder. You saw him kick down at me as he had kicked down at Props. You saw——"

"Yes—yes, I saw his face."

"His behaviour was more damning than I dared hope it would be. When I sent him up the ladder I knew he was planning how he would play the part of the horrified discoverer of the suicide. I thought he would very likely recognise the dummy—it was simply a weighted sack—and I wanted to see how he would react. I hardly dared hope he would do what he did."

"He didn't even look at it. He saw something that scraped the upper surface of the cloth and he thought it was the feet of the body. In his mind was the vivid picture of the swinging corpse and in the violent turbulence of his emotion he did not pause to look—did not want to look—— He gave his magnificent performance of horror-truck discovery and—recognised Props! An innocent man would have looked and seen at once that a weighted sack hung from a rope."

"I wonder he consented to go up the ladder."

"He couldn't refuse. I treated the unfortunate Simpson to a display of official suspicion. The little man was scared out of his life, and Gardener was reassured. To refuse would have been impossible."

"There seems," said Nigel, "so little motive for so big a risk."

"Not when you go into the case. If Surbonadier had blown the gaff, Gardener would have been scrapped by Saint. If his authorship of the article in the *Morning Express* had come out, Saint could and would have done him incalculable harm. You may depend upon it that Surbonadier had been bleeding him for pretty hefty sums. A drug addict gets through lots of money. And Surbonadier could have given Stephanie Vaughan some very nasty information about Felix Gardener. I wonder how much Gardener himself had told her. Enough to make her risk that visit to the flat. She's a courageous creature."

Nigel looked curiously at him.

"She attracts you very much, doesn't she?" he ventured.

Alleyn got up and stood looking out into the yard.

"When she's not being a leading lady, she does," he said coolly.

" You're a rum old fish."

" Think so? Come and have some lunch. I must get back to the Yard."

" I don't feel like eating," said Nigel.

" You'd better try."

They walked down the alley-way to the front of the theatre. The gigantic unicorn in steel and black glass glittered against its starry background. Alleyn and Nigel looked up at it for a moment.

" There's one unique feature in this case," said Alleyn.

" What's that?"

" Thanks to you I was able to watch the murder in comfort from a fifteen-and sixpenny stall provided by the murderer."

He held up his stick to a taxi and they drove away in silence.